She Will Rise Again

She Will Rise Again

Cheryl Fonteh

November Media Publishing, Chicago IL.
Copyright © 2017 Cheryl Fonteh

This book is a work of fiction. The names, characters, places and incidents are products of the writer's imagination or have been used fictitiously and are not to be construed as real. Any resemblance to persons, living or dead, actual events, locales or organizations is entirely coincidental.

Ordering Information:
Special discounts are available on quantity purchases by corporations, associations, and others. For details, contact the publisher at the email address above.

Printed in the United States of America
ISBN-13: 978-0-9990431-2-7 (print)

Acknowledgements

Many thanks to Almighty God for blessing me with so many amazing gifts. To my wonderful parents, Prof. and Prof. Mrs. Fonteh for encouraging me to pursue my dreams. My brothers, Terence and Herbert for making me dream BIG. Gabriella and Immanuel Umenei for their unending support and suggestions. The rest of my family for believing in me, and my amazing friends for reading drafts of my manuscript and pushing me to keep writing.

Dedication

To all who are going through a wilderness season in their life, all who are trying to figure out their purpose in life and all who are suffering from the consequences of a poorly made decision. Keep the faith and trust in God. There is something beautiful on the other side. "And we know that in all things, God works for the good of those who love Him, who have been called according to His purpose." Romans 8:28

One

Raelynn stood on the balcony of the third story building, gazing at the stars. It was fall, that particular time of the year when it was neither too hot nor too cold; the temperature was just right. She took a deep breath in, closed her eyes and smiled. It had rained earlier that day and the air smelled earthy and refreshing. She loved living in the suburbs. She would never trade this to live in New York City-- the city that never sleeps. Visiting the city was great when one was a tourist, but a chore when you actually lived there for more than a couple of weeks. She tried the whole living in the city thing for a while just after she got to New York. It was too much. She could not do it. There was never a single moment of peace, --it was congested and stuffy. During the summer, the trashcans the residents put out on the curb made the alleys stink badly. She was so happy to move to Jersey, even if it meant she had to commute forty-five minutes everyday to work. It was totally worth it.

It was a quiet night and all she heard were dogs barking in the distance. It was about 3:00 am and the city of Newark was asleep. A bad dream woke her up about an hour ago and for the life of her, she had not been able to fall back asleep. She tossed and turned for a while before wandering out onto the balcony.

In her dream she saw…

She shook her head. No. She should not be too worried about the dream. Dreams were just dreams, no matter how authentic they seemed. She was sure Josh was fine. She had not heard from him in a couple of weeks, but that was not unusual. Sometimes when Josh was pursuing a new deal with his clients, he would end up in a very remote place with them with poor mobile data and Wi-Fi. During these times, it was hard to get a hold of him for weeks. Other times, he was very bad at communicating. He was probably all right.

She really did need to get some sleep. Madame Josephine would not be happy if she showed up to work with bags under her eyes. As a model, she always had to look well rested and refreshed. Also, she needed to meet her personal trainer at 5:30 am, before she went for a run, got ready for work, and reported to the office by 9:00 am. Urgh! The pressure was real. She made a U-turn away from the balcony, walked back into her bedroom and closed the door leading to the balcony. Her room was filled with a soft yellow glow from one of the night lamps. She walked past her bed and went in the kitchen to pour a glass of almond milk. "Maybe it'll help me with my sleep," she thought. She put the milk in the microwave and heated it for about a minute. She sipped it slowly, while she surveyed the kitchen. It was a small, cozy kitchen with granite countertops and white cupboards.

There were three high chairs around the island and a bunch of mail stashed in one corner. She made a mental note to herself to go grocery shopping soon. She had pushed it off for the past couple of days. Her bowl of fruit on the island's countertop, which typically had an assortment of fruits in it, now only had one measly mango. Even her fridge was half-empty. After finishing her milk, she walked back to her bedroom and took off the bathrobe she had worn to go outside. She went into her closet to hang it up. She turned the light switch on and studied the closet space for a second. Her closet was huge--almost big enough to be a bedroom. It was befitting of a model. She had one wall shelved with shoes and another one that was filled with handbags. There were racks and racks of clothes in several sizes, styles, and colors. She was amazed at the amount of clothes she had obtained in the past six years. She landed on the shores of New York with basically nothing but the clothes she wore and a few personal items in a backpack.

Now as one of the top models in New York City, she bought a new outfit every time she attended a function, and she hardly ever wore the same outfit twice. If there was one thing she was really into, it was her clothes. It was the only thing she spent any money on, and she was very good at finding deals. Compared to most of her modeling colleagues, she had a pretty modest lifestyle. She lived in an ordinary one-bedroom apartment, did not go on exotic vacations and was not out partying every weekend. Plus, she did not own a car. She had a little mountain bike, which she sometimes rode to and from work and on the weekends. Hence, she was able to save a great deal of money over the past six years. Most of the money she saved, she sent to Josh. He graduated from an engineering school the year before. Thanks to all the capital she gave him, and with the help of his partner Anthony, Josh was able to start his own company. As a new company, it struggled the first couple of months. But now it was actually picking up speed and beginning to really thrive financially.

She turned off the light in the closet and walked over to her bed. It was a huge California King bed with a frame made of dark wood. She had a zillion pillows on it, which were turquoise and light pink; her favorite colors. Her bed sheets and comforter were Egyptian and as cozy as they could be. She slid off her slippers and sank down on the soft mattress. She looked at the gigantic mantel clock on her right wall, which read 3:20 am. She sighed, reached over to turn off her night lamp, and started fighting sleep again.

She hurried out of her apartment and rushed into the streets of Newark to catch the bus and shuttle to Manhattan. She waved quickly at the middle-aged Iranian guy in a donut shop she passed by on her way to work everyday. He had been working there for as long as she could remember. They had developed a little routine. Every morning when she walked by, he offered her a doughnut. And every morning she declined and offered him a dollar or two. Sometimes when she had time to spare, she stopped to chat with him for a few minutes. Over the past few years, she learned a lot about the man. Twenty years ago, he moved to the US with his newlywed wife. They struggled for a while to get on their feet. Raelynn could easily relate to his story. She too had struggled to make it when she came to the US. The man worked odd jobs until he was able to save up enough money to buy the donut shop, which was now flourishing. The couple had four kids--three girls and a boy. Their oldest kid was recently admitted into Brown University. Their son's acceptance into this Ivy League school thrilled him to no end. He rambled on and on about how smart his son was and how proud he and his wife were. They seemed like a really sweet family and Raelynn actually enjoyed hearing him brag about his son.

On the commute to work, she thought about how long it had been since she had a donut or any form of processed sugar. All she ate for breakfast was unseasoned broccoli and boiled egg whites. Lunch and dinner were very similar fares: boiled vegetables, some protein and very little carbs. She missed her greasy and tasty Cameroonian meals--sliced fried plantain, also known as dodo, ndole (bitter leaf and peanut soup), eru, puff-puff, etc. She was tired of this model life and would not mind having some extra meat on her bones. She gave herself a mental shake again, "Madame Josephine would never allow it."

The first time they met, Madame Josephine intimidated her. Raelynn was only eighteen at the time. It had been seven years since then, but if she was honest, Madame Josephine still scared her to death. She had three more years left on her contract, and then her debt would be paid and she would be free to do whatever she liked and eat whatever she wanted.

"Raelynn," a deep male voice barked, as soon as she walked into the Moreau building. "You're very late. Madame Josephine is in her office. You don't want to keep her waiting."

"Oh for crying out loud, she was only about a minute late," Raelynn thought as she mentally rolled her eyes. She would never actually roll her eyes at Derrick. He was second-in-command to Madame Josephine and he also petrified her. Derrick Lance was the all-American dream man; tall with wavy, dark blond hair, physically fit, blue eyes and a face that seemed to be sculpted by a talented artist. Women always threw themselves at him. However, there was something very sinister in his eyes. Whenever Raelynn looked into them, she shuddered a little. But over the past couple of weeks, there was something different in his eyes when he looked at her. He had the same expression a cat had when it looked at a delicious bowl of cream.–At first, she thought she imagined it until the other girls she worked with commented on how lucky she was to have caught his eyes. She felt her skin crawl.

"Of course Derrick. I'm heading over there right now" she replied and quickly walked past him. She felt his eyes bore into her back as she sashayed towards the elevators, through stands of clothes that were placed there for the models to use for their fittings. As head of the agency, Madame Josephine's office was on the top floor of the 40th floor building.

Josephine Moreau started her modeling career in Paris. She came to the United States in her late thirties and started the Moreau Modeling Agency in New York. Over the past fifteen years, she built quite a name for herself. She managed to find the most talented and beautiful models from all over the country to work for her. Companies all over the country vied to work with one of her models to shoot commercials. A handful of her models even starred in some Hollywood movies.

Raelynn gave a light tap on the door before walking into Madame's plush office. The desk, drawers, and cabinets were all made from jet-black mahogany. Almost everything else in her office was white in color: from the couch in the center of the room, to the carpet, to the revolving chairs, one on each side of her desk. She had a magnificent art collection on her right wall. There were paintings from great artists like Van Gogh, Grant Wood, Claude Monet Madame and Michelangelo Buonarroti. There were no pictures of family or friends anywhere in her office, which left most of her employees wondering if she had any family at all. Or maybe she was very private. Either way, Madame Josephine never talked about her family on any occasion. On the left side of the office, there was a door, which opened up to a breathtaking terrace. There was a long rectangular pool of water leading all the way to the edge of the building, with a fountain at its center. On either side of the pool were two steps with potted plants. Birds were always chirping softly in the background. The terrace's relaxing atmosphere would almost make you forget you were in the middle of Manhattan.

Madame Josephine was standing behind her desk by the window, which had a breathtaking view of the city. From her office, there was a good view of 5th Avenue and you saw all the way to Central Park. At Raelynn's entrance, she turned and gave her a crooked smile.

"*Voila*, Raelynn. Please have a seat," she said. It was not uncommon for her to interlace her English with French. Most of her customers found it quite endearing.

Raelynn took a seat on one of the revolving chairs, as Madame Josephine walked back to her desk and sat down. Madame Josephine was a petite woman with jet-black hair, green eyes, and a sweet angelic baby face. She was still slender and toned like all of her models. Though she was almost forty-five, she did not look a day over thirty-five. She did a great job of taking care of herself and maintaining her appearance. Plus, she was always impeccably dressed. Today she wore a knee-length dark green dress, which was sleeveless and folded asymmetrically on the bottom.

"Hi Madame Josephine. I apologize for my tardiness," Raelynn said, sitting up straighter in her seat. Madame Josephine waved her hand in dismissal.

"That's alright, *Ma Petite*. How are you today? You look a little tired. You need your beauty sleep,

Ma Chérie." Before Raelynn came up with a response, Madame Josephine continued, "I was very pleased with your work on the last assignment in Los Angeles. Not only were you able to get Mr. Jones' credit card information from his wallet, but you also managed to copy his personal data from his phone, as well as get his fingerprints. And you did all of this after talking to the fellow for less than ten minutes. You made the work for the rest of the team a piece of cake. *Magnifique*!!!"

Raelynn gave Madame Josephine a sly smile. One of the reasons she got the details from the man so swiftly was because he was a sleaze ball and she wanted to get out of his presence as quickly as she could. In the brief time they talked, he managed to use the most derogatory and racial slurs possible. He also told her one of his deranged fantasies involving black women. In all her years as a model, Raelynn heard a ton of disturbing comments and remarks about both women and African Americans, but Mr. Jones somehow managed to top them all.

To Madame Josephine, she was more than just a model. Her best use of Raelynn happened when she was off duty as a model. There were a few times Raelynn felt guilty about conning people. Some of them seemed like really nice and genuine people. But she had to do what she had to do. As one of the models from the Moreau Company, Raelynn was invited to several events across the country like parties, fund-raisers, pageants, etc. At these functions, she flirted with a chosen target, while using a highly sophisticated device Madame Josephine gave to her (she called it *Twista*) to steal as much information from the target as she could. *Twista* could access data from any device it was connected to. This included deleted messages or emails, PINs and passwords. However, the information *Twista* collected was not in any particular order, and the computer tech guys at the Moreau Company had to sift through all the data to fish out any valuable information. It could take a couple of months for them to go through every email or message to figure out which passwords matched which bank accounts. Although they always figured it out, Raelynn was not exactly sure how it was done. The computer techs cleared a good chunk of someone's bank accounts and then removed all traces leading back to them.

When she had an operation, she first shrewdly picked the target's phone, wallet or both without them noticing and went to the bathroom. She then used *Twista* to steal the information from the phone, and take pictures of the credit cards. Afterwards, she returned the items to the target without them noticing. It took skill and a lot of luck to pull off each operation successfully. Having hundreds of people at any of these events was both a blessing and a curse. Since there were so many people, there was always a chance someone would see her and call the cops. On the other hand, since there were many people chatting and drinking wine with a lot of buzz and pomp, no one person paid particular attention to her, which made her job easier. She was still scared to death about getting caught one day and spending years in prison. But her fear of what Madame

Josephine would do to her far exceeded her fear of getting caught by the cops.

Two

S he first met Madame Josephine seven years ago, Shortly after she had arrived New York. Raelynn arrived on a ship from the coast of West Africa as an illegal immigrant. She narrowly avoided deportation at the port of entry in New York.

The only reason she made it through was because she met a fellow Cameroonian who worked at the Port, named Paul Ade. Paul felt sorry for her and begged his colleagues to grant her a temporary two-week visa until she received the appropriate papers. Due to all the protests and violence in Cameroon, Paul helped her obtain an Asylum status. Paul had been of immense help to her during her first few days in the United States and Raelynn was eternally grateful for him. He even suggested she stay at his home for a few weeks, until she sorted things out. Unfortunately, Paul's Nigerian wife, Adama, had violently opposed the idea. She insinuated Paul was having an affair with Raelynn and threatened to divorce him if he continued to interact with her. Naturally, Paul was not going to break up his marriage for someone he just met. So after he helped Raelynn get a Permanent Resident card, he left her to her own devices.

With the little savings she had, Raelynn was able to pay for a little room at Motel 6 for four weeks until all her savings ran out. After the money was gone, she was penniless and was kicked out of the motel. During that time, she tried everything to find a job. She applied to work in all kinds of places; from being a janitor, to being a waitress at a fast food restaurant, to working in customer service at a grocery store/pizza joint and so on; all to no avail. No one wanted to hire her. She was finally offered a job to clean dishes at some Chinese fast food joint. By that time, she was living on the streets of New York City for almost three weeks. She spent most of her days roaming Central Park. But at night, it was really rough there. So to avoid being assaulted, she spent her nights riding on one of New York City transit buses or trains.

However, her new boss soon made it clear that he wanted more from her than washing dishes. In plain terms, he wanted her to be his side-chick. To make matters worse, the man was married with five kids. There were many things Raelynn would do for money, but sleeping with a fella was not one of them. She shot him down and told him he was a pig. Of course, the guy fired her on the spot. She walked out onto the street, feeling hungry, dejected and alone. She walked back to Central Park, sunk down onto a bench, pulled out a Snickers candy bar from her backpack and ate it slowly, contemplating her miserable life. This was her only meal for the day. Maybe leaving Cameroon was not the best idea. At least back home, she was able to work as a hairdresser and always had something to eat. She wondered how Josh was faring--probably a lot better than she was. Josh was very resourceful and even with all the political unrest in Cameroon; he figured a way to take care of himself. Unknown to her, a lady was watching her as she ate. This particular lady had been watching her for the past couple of days.

Once Raelynn was done with her Snickers, the lady walked up, and sat down on the bench next to her. Raelynn started to rise before the lady firmly said, "No. Please sit." Raelynn sat back down and they sat there in silence for a while. The lady then added, "I'm willing to offer you a job. If you are interested."

Raelynn's heart leaped in her chest. She turned and looked at this attractive lady who was dressed in a black high-waist skirt, a red blouse and five-inch heels. How could fate be this kind to her? There had to be a catch somewhere. If there was anything she learned in this life, you do not get something for nothing. She squinted her eyes and continued to look at the woman suspiciously. "What kind of job?"

"A model." The lady responded. Still not looking at her.

Raelynn's mouth dropped. "Say what now?" She looked down at herself and almost laughed--she came to the United States with one pair of black jeans, a few T-shirts and a jacket. The jeans were so worn out now that the color changed from jet-black to grey. Even the pink T-shirt she wore faded with a loose hem. The grey tennis shoes she wore were now brown from dirt. She was very sure she smelled like skunk, as she had not showered for almost three days. Her only decent feature was her hair. She braided it just before leaving Cameroon and it still looked a little decent. Was the woman crazy? In what universe was she good enough to be a model?

"Me?" Raelynn asked as she pointed a finger to herself. "You must be kidding."

The lady now turned and looked at her. It was a cold, calculating look that would chill a 6-foot tall man to the bones. "Do I look like I'm kidding?"

Raelynn swallowed. Looks like the lady was serious after all.

"Why me," she whispered?

"Because in spite of your outward appearance right now, I know beauty when I see it. Your face and body figure are perfect to be a model."

Raelynn was genuinely surprised. She never thought of herself like that before. Most of her folk back home complained she was too skinny and needed to put on a few pounds to look like a woman. Despite the fact that she had many suitors back home, she did not think she was particularly attractive. Sure, men called her beautiful all the time, but she always felt they said it to every other girl they met.

"What kind of model? Anything with nude pictures?"

"You don't have to if you'd rather not."

"So all I have to do is wear pretty and expensive clothes and take pictures?"

"Pretty much. Just one more thing."

"Here we go," Raelynn thought. This is the catch. "What's that?"

"When you go to high function events, I'll need you to do something for me."

"What's that?" Raelynn asked again.

"I cannot discuss that right now, it's personal. You'll have to agree to work for me first."

She shook her head. There had to be something sinister about this job offer. No matter how desperate, hungry and tired she was, she would not fall for it.

She replied calmly, "I'm sorry Madame. I can't do that."

The lady did not argue with her and simply said, "Have it your way then." She stood up. "But just in case you change your mind, here's my card."

The lady thrust one of her business cards into Raelynn's hands and briskly walked away. Raelynn looked at the card, which read:

Josephine Moreau
Founder and CEO of Moreau Modeling Agency
760 5th Avenue
New York, NY 10153
(212) 366-1400

She put it away in one of the pockets in her backpack. Just in case.

The next couple of weeks were rough. She did not catch a break. She managed to get a few menial jobs, but it was only a matter of days before someone at her new job, typically the boss or manager, started sexually harassing her. The last place she worked was at a laundry mat. She had been there for three days when the pompous manager, a pudgy Caucasian man in his late thirties, grabbed her in a back room and started inappropriately touching her. When she objected, the man forced his mouth down on hers. She was never so mad in her entire life. She gathered all the strength she could muster and kneed him hard in the groin. When he doubled over in pain, she put her hands on his shoulders and kneed him in the face. She pushed him aside, quickly collected her personal items, and ran out the room and then out of the building. Of course, she never returned.

Still homeless, she used the little money she made to buy food. She refused to go out on the street and beg like most homeless people did. Most of the people in the city did not pay attention to the beggars anyway. Her money was running out fast and she was running out of options. To make matters worse, the seasons had gradually changed from fall to winter and the temperatures outside were now freezing. The first night it snowed she thought she would freeze to death. It was then she decided to find that lady, Ms. Moreau, and take her up on her offer. She was willing to do anything now except sleep with any man or beg. The next morning she was shivering as she walked up to the Moreau's offices on 5th Avenue. The security guy refused to believe she had any business with Ms. Moreau and kicked her out of the building. Raelynn did not blame him. She caught a glimpse of herself from the glass door and knew she looked a wreck. She sat down on the steps in front of the building and waited patiently for Ms. Moreau to exit through the door. Ms. Moreau did not come out of the building until about 1:00 pm and she was accompanied by two models and a bodyguard. When Raelynn saw her, she rushed up to her and yelled.

"Ms. Moreau. It's me. The girl from Central Park."

Ms. Moreau stopped in her tracks, turned her head and gave her a look from head to toe. The bodyguard tried to shush Raelynn away, but Ms. Moreau held up her hand and said, "*Ca va,*" to the bodyguard, "Leave her alone." The bodyguard stepped back, as Raelynn stepped closer to her.

"*Advancer sans moi.* I'll catch up with you later." Ms. Moreau whispered to her companions. The two models nodded, looked at Raelynn with disgust and strolled off. Ms. Moreau gave Raelynn another look from head to toe before nodding towards the door.

"Let's talk inside, shall we?" she asked and started walking back towards the building. Raelynn followed her closely. When she passed by the security guard, Raelynn almost gave him a smirk of satisfaction, but decided against it. The room was abuzz with models and designers running back and forth. Ms. Moreau took her through a side door, away from the crowd, and led her into a small office. The office was poorly lit and sparsely decorated. It had a desk, a leather chair and two white industrial café chairs. Ms. Moreau gently shut the door behind her and walked over to the leather chair behind the desk, sat down and crossed her legs. Raelynn was still standing by the door, grateful to be out of the cold. Ms. Moreau motioned her to take a seat in one of the industrial café chairs. Raelynn nervously sat down, still shivering a little.

"So… *Ma Petite*, you reconsidered my offer?" Ms. Moreau asked.

Raelynn nodded slowly. She had no choice. But she had to set something straight.

"I won't have to take nude pictures, right?"

"No."

"Or sleep with anyone?"

"No."

"Or harm anyone?"

"Not exactly."

Raelynn nodded again. She could deal with that. "Ok then. I accept your offer."

"That's all good. But before we sign a contract, let me make one thing clear," Ms. Moreau said uncrossing her legs, leaning forward and placing both her elbows on the desk, while staring into Raelynn's eyes with a cold green stare. "I expect absolute loyalty from my employees. I will not be crossed. If you sign this contract, you'll have to work for me for ten years. After that, you are free to do as you please. If you ever, ever, try to leave before that time, you will regret it. Is that clear?"

At that instant, Raelynn knew in her gut despite Ms. Moreau's sweet appearance from the outside, she could be a vengeful and vindictive woman. She had no other choice but to say yes. She just hoped she would be able to carry out the other requirements of the job Ms. Moreau mentioned, and wondered what those requirements could possibly be.

She nodded quickly, *"Oui* Ms. Moreau."

"Oh you speak French? *Magnifique.* But you'll address me as Madame Josephine henceforth. *Tu as compris?"*

Raelynn nodded again. Madame Josephine then pulled out a document from one of her drawers and pointed where to sign. After they had both signed, Madame Josephine gave her a copy of the contract and kept the original.

"It's all settled then. Welcome to the family."

"Ummm thank you Ma'am. Words can't express how…"

"Tiene ca." Madame Josephine interrupted her quickly and offered her a huge stack of money. "This is a little advance from your first salary. Clean yourself up a bit. Buy some nice clothes and eat a decent meal. Looks like you haven't had one in months. Report back here tomorrow at 10:00 am. I'll tell the security guard to let you in."

Raelynn counted the money in her hands and her mouth dropped. It was $2,000. She felt like Julia Roberts in the classic movie, *Pretty Woman*, except she was not a prostitute.

Madame Josephine laughed at her expression. "Don't look so amazed. There will be a lot more coming. Hurry along *Ma Petite*. See you tomorrow."

Raelynn quickly rose to her feet and showered many thanks, as she opened the door and walked out of the room. The first thing she did when she left the building was walk to the nearest restaurant. She ordered lunch, which consisted of fried rice mixed with vegetables, a side of grilled salmon and some French fries. She was so famished that she ate like a deranged person. In less than five minutes, the food was all gone. She also ordered fruit and a slice of chocolate cheesecake for dessert. By the time she was done, she was so full her stomach hurt.

After leaving the restaurant, she went to a boutique and bought a bunch of clothes. She then headed to Marriot's Hotel and booked a room. As soon as she dropped her stuff by the corner of the bed, she undressed and got into the shower. She stood under the hot stream of water for almost half an hour before she lathered her skin with soap. She felt reborn as she stepped out of the shower and dried off with one of the many towels the hotel provided. She put on one of the outfits she just bought, fell onto the bed and slid off into a deep sleep.

***

She was now very good at what she did though. Over the past couple of years, she had never been caught. If she was honest with herself, there were times she enjoyed the thrill of the operations.

After she stole the information from her targets, she delivered them to Madame Josephine who then gave the information to a group of software hackers that also worked for her. Raelynn had no idea who the hackers were and the hackers had no idea who stole the information. Madame Josephine liked to keep the various subdivisions of her gang separate and blinded each of them from the other person. Raelynn did not even know if she was the only model who stole information from targets. All she knew was whenever she delivered personal information about a target, the hackers waited several months, even years before they wreaked havoc on the person's finances. By this time, they probably forgot about their encounter with Raelynn and would not be able to trace their loss of funds back to her or the Moreau Company.

"It was my pleasure Ma'am," Raelynn said after a brief pause. "That slime of a man had it coming."

"You know it *Ma Cherie*. I appreciate all the work you do here. As a token, here is a bonus check for you. Take the day off. Go to a spa or something. *Amuse toi*. I will debrief you about your next assignment on Monday."

Raelynn looked down at the check Madame Josephine handed her. Her eyes lit up when she saw the number of zeros on the check. Though Madame Josephine was a very ruthless businesswoman and demanded absolute loyalty from her gang of thieves, she was also very generous to them. In addition to her normal salary, every now and then, Madame Josephine also gave her a hefty bonus check.

Raelynn thanked her and immediately left the building and caught a train back to Jersey. She checked her Facebook and Whatsapp messages; still nothing from her brother Josh. Though she tried not to worry, she would not be at peace until she heard back from him. She told him several times to send her a signal every couple of weeks, so she didn't worry. But boys!!! Did they ever listen? She glanced at her unread messages on Whatsapp. One of them was from Franck, one of her closest friends. She clicked on the message, *'Yo, why have you thrown me nahhh? I don call u sotey tire.* Call me back.' Franck was her neighbor and playmate when Raelynn was growing up in Santa, a small town in Cameroon, West Africa. Though she left Cameroon seven years ago, they remained close friends. They often communicated in Pidgin English, one of the unofficial languages spoken in Cameroon.

'*Been busy ma man. Weti di happen* (what's up),' Raelynn replied. 'Have you heard from Josh recently?' Franck replied almost immediately, 'Nope I haven't heard from him in a while. Things were rough for a while out here. *But the place di calm down now. I sure sey ei still dey for country* (village).'

After the last president of Cameroon who was in power for almost half a century had passed away almost ten years ago, the country was thrown into a state of turmoil. There were *coup d'états* (violent overthrow of an existing government by a small group) every few months. It was during one of those *coup d'états* that she left Cameroon and eventually found herself on the streets of New York.

She and Josh were running away from some rebels towards a ship bound for Accra, Ghana. Unfortunately, one bullet hit Josh on his upper thigh and he couldn't run anymore. She stopped to help him finish the last couple of meters, but the rebels closed in on them and he urged her to go on without him. "There was no sense in both of us getting captured," he said. With tears in her eyes, she left him there and made it to the ship.

That was the last time she saw her beloved twin brother, Josh. She didn't hear from him for six months. Then one day, Franck called her and put him on the phone. She cried out of relief when she heard his voice. She tried to help him fly out of the country several times during the first few years of their separation. Unfortunately, the country developed very stringent rules about leaving the country and she never succeeded. About a year ago, the political tension subsided and they made plans for him to visit. He was supposed to fly out to New York City in a month.

During all this time, they kept in touch frequently, except when he went off the grid for one reason or another for months at a time. She hadn't heard from him in two weeks. Although he has gone off the grid for longer periods of time in the past, this time she had a sinking feeling that something happened to him.

She shook her head again to clear her thoughts, as she decided not to worry about Josh. "He'll turn up somewhere," she thought, "He always does." She continued texting Franck and a few of her other friends in Cameroon, till she got home, fell on her bed and crashed.

Three

Bryan stared at his watch for the tenth time within the past fifteen minutes. He was not the most patient guy in the world and his wife was always late; even on their anniversary!!! Sometimes he felt she was late on purpose, just to rile him up. He took a deep breath in and took a sip of water. He glanced at his phone and was tempted to text her again. He decided against it and took another sip of water. He was a stickler for punctuality. He did not understand how someone could be almost an hour late to an important occasion. When someone kept him waiting, he genuinely felt disrespected. It took his wife a long while to understand that. In the first couple of weeks of their marriage, they fought several times about her tardiness. He remembered on one particular occasion, after a fight, they went for almost two weeks without speaking to each other. They talked about the issue for hours and came to a compromise. He promised to be more patient, and she promised not to be more than fifteen minutes late for a rendezvous. So far, she kept her end of the bargain. She was usually no more than ten minutes late when they met up someplace. She let the ball drop today by being almost half an hour late. This was their anniversary and he promised himself not to get worked up for any reason.

Five minutes later, he looked up and saw her walk from across the room. She waved gently and gave him a broad smile. Wow, she looked stunning! She wore a long red dress that fit her slender physique perfectly and glowed against her caramel skin. Her long wavy hair was styled impeccably, and so was her makeup. She had high cheekbones, a relatively long chin (which he loved to tease her about) and the most beautiful brown eyes he had ever seen. He knew looking good was part of her job and it is what made her successful, but she never failed to take his breath away. She was beautiful! Beneath that sophisticated and alluring exterior, she was the most caring and down-to-earth person he had ever met. She was the kind of person who would drop everything and run to help him if he asked. He could talk with her about anything. On several occasions, they spent hours and hours talking about everything and nothing at the same time.

As she walked up to him, he grinned and stood up to greet her.

"Hi Babe, happy anniversary," he said, pulling her into his arms for a warm hug and a kiss.

"Hi Baby, happy anniversary," she responded. "I'm so sorry I'm late. I couldn't find the keys in my bag, so I had to…"

"That's alright." He gently interrupted her. "Don't worry about it. I'm just glad to be here with you." He gave her a sweeping glance from head-to-toe before adding, "You look good, Darling."

"Aww, thanks Babe," Raelynn replied sweetly, while beaming. He never failed to compliment her, and she never got tired of hearing it. "You look dapper yourself, Mr. Handsome."

She reached to adjust his neck collar and slowly ran her hands down his jacket. He donned a perfectly tailored dark grey suit with a salmon-colored shirt. The top three buttons were casually unbuttoned. "He must have gotten a haircut," she thought. The small goatee and mustache were now neatly trimmed--just the way she liked it.

Bryan grinned, "Gotta keep up with you Hun. Can't be hanging out with you looking like a hippie."

He pulled up a seat for her. After she sat down, he picked up a huge bouquet of red roses from under the table and gave them to her.

"Awwwwwwwwwwww," Raelynn exclaimed and leaned over the cozy booth to give him another kiss. "Thanks Babe! These are lovely. You are too sweet."

As the waiter poured water into their glasses, they laughed and talked about each other's day, like they did everyday, either via phone or in person.

They lived in separate apartments to keep their relationship a secret; especially from everyone who worked in the Moreau Company. Very few people knew they were together, and even fewer ones knew they were married. The restaurant Bryan chose was in Queens, an area where they were unlikely to run into anyone affiliated with Moreau Company.

Bryan started talking about a small Bible study group meeting he attended the night before. The Bible verse they studied was 1 Corinthians 13, which is the passage on love. They meditated on 1 Corinthians 13:4-7 of the New Living Translation (NLT): "Love is patient and kind. Love is not jealous or boastful or proud or rude. It does not demand it's own way. It is not irritable, and it keeps no record of being wronged. It does not rejoice about injustice but rejoices whenever the truth wins out. Love never gives up, never loses faith, is always hopeful and endures every circumstance." The leader of the group probed them to replace the word love in this passage with God. "God is patient and kind; God never keeps a record of wrong and so on." Bryan had never thought about this passage that way before and he was blown away by how well it fit.

A co-worker invited him to church about six weeks ago. Out of sheer curiosity, he decided to go. He had gone to church a couple of times before that-- usually on Christmas, New Year, Easter, a wedding or a funeral. No one in his family was particularly religious. Bryan did not expect the sermon that day to be so powerful. The pastor preached about Saul's conversion story in Acts 9 and how Jesus appeared to him and completely changed his life. He talked about how the Holy Spirit convicts people when they least expect it, and how the Holy Spirit has the power to transform lives.

"So many people," the pastor said, "Were on their way to destruction because they refused to listen to the voice of the Holy Spirit. So are we going to wait until the Holy Spirit knocks us off our feet and strips us down or are we going to listen to that voice in our hearts, that is calling us back to Jesus?"

It was almost like the preacher was speaking directly to him, which was absurd because Bryan had never heard of or seen the guy before. It had to be something else. Bryan was so convicted that by the end of the sermon, when the pastor made the altar call, he walked down to the front of the church where the pastor and the worship band stood, and gave his life to Christ. Some time after, he bought a Bible, joined a small Bible study group and became passionate about his new faith.

Raelynn found it fascinating to hear him talk about his newfound love for Christ. She did not grow up religious either. As a child, her mom took her and Josh to church every Sunday, but it was more out of habit than anything else. She stopped going to church after her mother passed away. However, she always thought this Jesus Christ sounded like a pretty cool guy. She believed there was some "higher power" out there, but this whole business about one guy dying for and saving all of mankind sounded like a hoax to her. Nevertheless, she did not try to argue with Bryan when he spoke about Christianity, because she knew it had become important to him. She just smiled and nodded politely at him whenever he was on the topic.

Bryan stopped talking when the waiter brought an appetizer of olives and pistachio bruschetta that he ordered while waiting for her. They both moaned a little as they took their first bite.

"Mmmmmmmm, this is so good Babe," Raelynn commented as she took another bite. "I wish I could eat more."

"C'mon Babe, live a little. It's our one-year anniversary. Maybe you can forget about your crazy diet, just for today?"

Raelynn shook her head, "You know I can't Babe. I can only have a little. If it were up to you, I'd be 50 pounds heavier." After another bite or two, she resolutely put down her fork. Bryan leaned over and gave her another forkful, and then another. He kept prodding her to taste more until she ate almost as much as he had.

"Mmm, enough," she finally said when he offered her another bite. She swatted him playfully on the arm. "I'm gonna have to spend more time in the gym tomorrow to burn off these extra calories. You are a bad influence."

"Me???" Bryan exclaimed, as he put his hand on his chest somewhat dramatically. "You are the one who was a bad influence from the very first day we met. Or have you forgotten?"

Raelynn chuckled and reached out to take one of his hands in hers, "Of course not, Darling. How could I forget? That night is unforgettable."

Three years ago

It was a beautiful Chicago spring night. He was at an all white boat party with top businessmen from all over the country. Bryan was sent there as a representative from his father's company, OILBIKO. His father, Honorable David Abayomrunkoje Okoye, was a big international oil tycoon with offices in the States, Nigeria, and several other countries. He was currently valued at $4.4 billion. As his oldest and only son, Bryan owned a considerable share of OILBIKO and managed the United States' branch, while his dad focused on the branch in Nigeria.

Many celebrities and models were also invited to the party, and Raelynn was amongst them. She was not on the boat for fun and games. She was there on business, which in this case meant stealing information from her target's phone. She received her instructions from Derrick and he was pretty clear-- find the Nigerian oil guy, cozy up to him, steal as much information as you can, avoid contact with anyone else, leave the boat and meet him back at the Trump Tower lobby. The instructions were standard. Raelynn did not understand why Derrick was fussing over her. This was her fourth year working with Madame Josephine and she knew how these things went down.

As usual, she conducted extensive research on her target prior to the party and knew almost everything about him; from the last person he dated to where he was born.

The party started without a hitch. The DJ was popping and everyone was having a good time, except for Raelynn, who could not find her target. She sipped her Champagne slowly as she edged her way through the crowd, trying to find him. She talked to one or two people along her way, so as not to appear overly rude or snobbish. After about an hour, she decided he was not on the boat. She cursed under her breath, as she climbed down the stairs to the lower deck. There were a handful of people hanging out there, mostly cozy couples. She saw a guy with his back to her who looked liked her target, standing at the stern end of the boat. As she walked closer, she realized it was indeed Bryan Okoye. She was surprised to find him by himself when the party was roaring with a buzz on the upper deck. Usually her targets were at the center of the party, drunk and obnoxious, with a bunch of beautiful women hanging on their arms, which made it easy for her to get close to them. She stood there for a few minutes before deciding the best way to approach him. Suddenly, he turned around and caught her staring at him. It is almost like he sensed someone was watching him.

"Oh dear," she thought to herself. "Quick, come up with some good excuse to explain why you were staring at him."

Even as she willed herself to speak, the words disappeared in her mouth. Both stood still for a few moments, staring at each other. Finally he cleared his throat and said, "Well, we could continue doing this all night, but is there anything I can help you with, Miss?"

Contrary to what she expected, there was no trace of a Nigerian accent in his tone. "Ummmm," she cleared her throat. "I was wondering if you were Bryan Okoye?"

"Yeah I am. And you are…"

"Raelynn Ngwa," she answered as she moved closer to give him a handshake. He smiled and shook her hand firmly. Up close, he was more handsome and taller than he appeared in pictures. His ebony dark skin glowed against the white casual outfit he was wearing. He looked like a model.

"Nice to meet you Raelynn. You look familiar. Were you the lady in that Bud Light commercial with the monkey?"

"Oh noooo." Raelynn whimpered and put a hand over her face; that was one of the worst commercials she had ever done. In the commercial, she walked in a ranch holding a can of Bud Light beer with a monkey perched on her shoulder. After taking one sip, she passed out. Then the monkey takes a sip of the beer and starts talking. He then forces the drink down her throat and she wakes up. She smiles and says, 'Drink Bud Light now for the ultimate experience.' It was ridiculous. The commercial made no sense whatsoever. The drink was supposed to both overwhelm and resuscitate her. Also, the monkey was the vilest animal she had ever seen. It did not cooperate at all. It bit her hand once or twice. She went to the hospital immediately after the shoot to get a Tetanus shot. Raelynn did the commercial because Madame Josephine ordered her to do it. Madame Josephine owed the CEO of Bud Light a favor and this was the only way he allowed her to pay him back. Raelynn's colleagues made fun of her for weeks after that commercial.

"You saw that?" she asked weakly.

He chortled. "Yeah I did. Who didn't? The commercial aired often on TV. I think there were also pictures of you and the monkey on a couple of billboards."

Raelynn groaned again and put her hands on either side of her face. "Oh my goodness. This is so embarrassing."

Bryan threw his head back and laughed. "There's nothing to be embarrassed about. You were great. I thought the ad's message was a little peculiar. That's the main reason why I remember it so well."

She gave him a little smile. "I know you are just saying that to make me feel better, but thanks anyway."

He shook his head, "Nahh, I'm serious. You played your part very well."

"Thanks again," she murmured. After a brief moment she added,

"I am fascinated with the work you and your father are doing with OILBIKO in the Delta region. The novel technique you guys use to drill oil--it's incredible."

He looked at her in surprise. Most girls her age were not interested in learning anything about his business. They usually talked about mundane things like their hair, their clothes, their boyfriends, their exes, etc. "Well it's mostly my father's work, but thanks anyway. I appreciate your interest. The technique isn't that novel. Several countries have used *'zipper frac'* technique for years. It's just the first time it's being done in West Africa. Are you by any chance Nigerian?"

"No, I'm not. I get that a lot. I am Cameroonian. You Nigerians are everywhere. There is a saying which goes, 'If you go somewhere and don't see a Nigerian, leave that area immediately. Because either the Nigerians came earlier, explored the area and found nothing, or they came and took away everything.'"

He laughed, "What can I say? We do good business." There was another brief pause, before he added, "So what are you doing hiding down here Miss Rae? A pretty girl like yourself is usually the life of the party."

Raelynn shrugged and leaned her elbows against the handrails, "I don't know. It just seems so peaceful down here. Look at that view, it's amazing."

Bryan also leaned his elbows on the rail and looked at the Chicago skyline, fading, as the boat drifted further away.

They stood there side by side talking and laughing for hours. They chatted like they were old friends. They talked about everything from politics, to food, to business, to music, to fashion, etc. Raelynn forgot about her assignment. She never clicked like this with anyone else before. The boat sailed across Lake Michigan for a few hours and was now heading back to shore. An idea suddenly popped into Raelynn's head and she asked, "Do you know what would be fun?"

Bryan shook his head. Even though he was a little wary of her at first, she now intrigued him. This was the only time he met someone like her at these events. A girl who was not just beautiful, but one who had brains too. He only came to these events every now and then, because it helped maintain the OILBIKO's social image. It would seem rude if he never showed up to any of the events his partners and associates invited him too. It did not matter if he interacted with them or not at these events; he just had to make an appearance. Meeting Raelynn was a pleasant surprise.

"We should go for a midnight dip in the lake."

He looked at her like she was deranged. "Are you serious? Nope, you are crazy."

"I hear it's very refreshing, and you feel reborn afterwards," she insisted.

"C'mon, that's white people stuff. We Africans don't do that. Can you even swim?"

Before she answered, the boat hit the shore. She put her purse aside and jumped into the invigorating water. She disappeared beneath it for a few moments. The rest of the party on the deck heard the splash and looked down to see what was going on. She emerged and shouted, "Whoot wooo!" The rest of the party responded, "Ayyyyyyyyeeeeee!"

Bryan stood there with an amused expression on his face. She beckoned for him to jump in too. He shook his head no again. She tried convincing him one more time and this time, against his better judgment, he put aside some of his personal items and jumped in. The crowd gave another round of applause and then everybody else at the party started jumping in the lake, as several lifeguards tried in vain to stop them. After a few moments, the party in the water became quite rowdy and a lady almost drowned, because she was drunk. The cops were called and rushed everyone out of the water. To get a complete police report, the cops questioned everyone. When the cops found out Raelynn and Bryan instigated the whole fiesta, they almost made them spend a night in jail. It was only because Bryan pleaded with them for over 45 minutes that they decided to only give each of them a warning.

"Well…you almost got us into some real trouble back there," Bryan said to her after they left the small office where the police officer interrogated them.

"Yeah, sorry about that. It was worth it though. I didn't expect everyone else to join us."

Bryan smirked, "Yup it was totally worth it. YOLO!" He screamed.

It was almost 4:30 am now and both of their shoulders were wrapped in small blankets the lifeguards gave them. It was an amazing night and Bryan did not want it to end just yet. He thought of inviting her back to his suite on Michigan Avenue, but it seemed tacky to him and he did not want her to get the wrong idea. So instead, he invited her to sit with him by the lake for a bit. They continued talking and before they knew it, the sun was rising. It was simply beautiful. Without saying a word, he took one of her hands in his and interlaced their fingers, as they watched the sunrise in a comfortable silence. Bryan was deciding if he should lean in to kiss her when she checked her phone. It had been buzzing all night and she had not read any of her messages, till just then. Her eyes widened with trepidation as she quickly stood up.

"I gotta go."

"Ummm okay. You want me to walk you to a cab or something?" he asked and also stood up.

"No, I'll be fine. Thank you." She started walking away when he gently grabbed her arm and turned her back around.

"I had a great time last night. When can I see you again?"

She slowly shook her head, "Never, I'm afraid."

"Why not?"

"It's complicated," she replied sadly.

"I'd love to hear the story," he persisted. Raelynn tried to disengage her arm from him, but to no avail.

"I'm sorry, I can't. Please let me go."

He let her go and she started walking away. After only taking a few steps, she turned around, walked back to him and gave him a brief, but sweet kiss. Then she turned back around and ran off.

***

Raelynn took another sip of her wine and smiled, "I honestly thought I'd never see you again."

"You sure made it difficult," Bryan replied and raised her fingers to his lips. "But fortunately for you, I'm a very persistent guy. Here's to us." He raised his glass and she followed suit.

"Here's to us Baby, and a lifetime of happiness," she answered and clinked their glasses.

"Before I forget, I have something for you," she added and reached down into her bag and pulled out a large parcel.

"Oh my goodness, how did you fit that in there?" he exclaimed. "You ladies can pull out anything from these handbags, can't you? One day you're gonna pull out a crock pot or something and I won't be surprised."

Raelynn chuckled and gave him the parcel.

"Thanks Babe," he said and leaned over to kiss her. "I didn't know we were doing this here. Mine is at home. Maybe I should wait to open it."

"It's ok. I was planning to give it to you later, but at the spur of the moment, I changed my mind. Open it."

"You sure? I feel bad."

"Awww Babe, don't be. Just open it."

He tore off the gift-wrapping and pulled out a painting, a Bible and an engraved pen. He immediately picked up the Bible. It was a Life Application Bible with a ton of footnotes and comments; basically, the best Bible for a new Christian. He opened the first page and read the small "From" label she had filled out

To the Love of my life,
Happy anniversary. The past three years with
you has been amazing. I'm so thankful for you
in my life. Meeting you was the best thing that
ever happened to me.
I'm so happy to see you so passionate about your new
faith.
I hope this helps with your journey as a Christian.

I love you more than words can express.
Wifey,
Rae

His eyes were shimmering with tears, as he looked up at her, "Babe…"

"Check out the rest," she gently urged.

He took a look at the painting and realized it was a painting of him, in his traditional Ibo attire. He took a picture like this the last time he was home in Lagos. The painting was stunning. Somehow the artist managed to bring life and character into the painting. It was so lifelike and looked almost exactly like him. He looked down to read the artist's name and saw her signature and someone else's scribbled at the bottom right corner.

"Wait, I don't understand. If I'm not mistaken, this is your signature. But you don't paint!" he exclaimed.

"Or do I?" she asked slyly, as she put her elbow on the table and rested her chin on her fist.

"I don't understand this Babe. How did you do this?"

"Well, I started taking painting classes a couple of weeks ago." He gaped at her. "My instructor and I painted it together. I wanted to surprise you," she continued.

He was visibly taken aback. "I had no idea Rae. This is incredible. Come here," he said with emotion and pulled her to her feet, as he stood up.

"You are so amazing. I love you, Rae," he added as he wrapped his arms tightly around her and kissed her.

Four

The few other people in the small cozy restaurant cheered and clapped as they kissed. They continued kissing for a few more moments, lost in their own little world. When they finally pulled apart, he gave her another kiss on the cheek before sitting down again. Raelynn was about to sit down when she saw Derrick from the corner of her eye. No, no, no!!! It could not be. What could he possibly be doing in this part of town? She turned around to make sure she was not imagining things. Their eyes met from across the room and he gave her a treacherous smirk. He was sitting at the other end of the room, apparently on a date with some blond who was busy chatting away.

"What was she going to do now?" she wondered. She spent the past three years carefully keeping her relationship with Bryan hidden from anyone at Moreau Company. Now the very last person who should know she was involved with Bryan Okoye just saw her making out with him in the middle of a restaurant. This was the worst possible thing that could have happened.

"Babe? Babe? Are you ok?"

She snapped back into reality and nodded, "Yeah, I'm fine."

"You zoned out on me a little. Is it because of the kiss? I'm sorry. I got a little carried away." When she did not say anything, he continued. "I know you like keeping our relationship on the down low, because of your boss and the modeling crew, and it somehow being bad for the business. We've been married for a year and together for almost three years. I'm sure they'll understand and even be happy for you, if you just tell them."

"If only he knew the whole story," she thought with amusement. He did not know the extent of her dealings with Madame Josephine. He believed she was simply a model. She never bothered to explain her whole involvement in the company. If she had, he probably would not have married or even gone out with her. Getting involved with any other person would have been fine by Madame Josephine. But getting involved with a target, one she was sent to extort and failed--now that was a problem. After she failed her mission, Madame Josephine sent different girls after him, but none succeeded. For reasons they could not understand, the young Mr. Okoye became extremely more secure and never carried his phone at big events. Madame Josephine was very upset about this and for the life of her, she could not understand why he was more security conscious all of a sudden.

Raelynn knew why. After their first meeting, she sent him an anonymous tip about someone trying to steal information from his phone. He heeded the advice and had taken precautions.

Now that Derrick saw her with him, it would not take a genius to put two and two together to figure out who tipped Bryan off. There was no telling what Madame Josephine might do when she found out. "Ohhh, this was bad. So bad."

"Rae? Rae?" she heard Bryan calling her again, as she snapped out of her thoughts. She wished she could shake off this feeling of dread and continue with their lovely dinner. But she could not. There were only a handful of times, she was truly scared. This topped them all.

"I'm sorry Babe. I just got a little distracted about something," she finally answered back and gave him a forced smile.

"You know you can tell me anything Babe. I…" Bryan started, but was interrupted by the petite brunette waitress who arrived with their meals.

"Here we go," she said cheerily as she set down the plates. "Enjoy. If you need anything else, just let me know. Okay?"

They both thanked the waitress. As soon as she left, Raelynn added

"Trust me Babe, I'm fine."

"But she was not fine," Bryan thought. Throughout the rest of the meal, she continued to be distracted and withdrawn. She was lost in her thoughts. She tried her best to hide it, but Bryan knew something was up. He was not an idiot. He wondered what had gotten into her head after the kiss to make her withdraw like this. He knew she did not like public displays of affection very much, because Madame Josephine thought it was bad for her brand or something. It did not completely make sense to him, but he was willing to play along.

It could not be the kiss though. She did not seem to mind it at all. WOMEN!!! Rae had her issues, but he never saw her go from 0 to 60 in less than two seconds, like this. Something really serious was bothering her and she refused to share it with him. He ran his hand over his hair with a look of frustration on his face.

After they finished their meal and sent for the check, Raelynn said, "Babe if you don't mind, I would like to spend the night at my apartment tonight."

"You mean us?"

"No, I meant just me." She corrected. His chest fell.

"Ummm why?"

"I feel a little off. I don't want to rub off my sour mood on you."

He reached over and gently touched her arm, "Rae, we are married. I signed up for all of you. When you are happy, sad, feeling off, or any other mood. I want all of you. I'm not running away because you feel off."

For reasons he could not understand, this statement filled her eyes with tears.

"Awww Babe. You are so sweet," she said softly and laid a hand on his cheek. "Sorry for spoiling the mood of the evening."

"That's okay. We have many more anniversaries to celebrate. I'm just worried about you. Are you sure everything is alright?"

She slowly nodded and stood up as the waitress brought back their receipt.

"Let's get you home," he said. As she slowly walked out of the restaurant, she tried to avoid looking at Derrick, but she could not help it. When she reached the door, she shot a glance in his direction and saw him watching her. He gave her a little nod with his chin, as she turned her gaze away and left.

It was about 2:00 am when Raelynn heard her phone buzz with an incoming text. She was not able to sleep since they got to her apartment. Bryan gave her a massage, ran a bath for her with candles, and brought her tea--all to lighten her mood. He was always so caring and thoughtful. Under other circumstances, that would have done the trick. Tonight nothing could. He finally went to sleep after midnight, while Raelynn tossed and turned on her side of the bed.

The text simply read, 'Meet in front of the Rockefeller Center at 6:00 am.'

She was both glad and petrified he texted her so soon. On one hand, it probably meant he was not planning to tell Madame Josephine about her secret. On the other hand, he could blackmail her. "Whatever he wanted from her would be far better than Madame Josephine finding out about Bryan," she thought. "What if he wanted her to sleep with him? Oh my goodness, no! She would never do that.

There must be something else he wanted from her." With these thoughts, she continued tossing and turning the entire night.

Although she arrived at the Rockefeller Center five minutes early, he was already there waiting for her. Bryan was still asleep when she left so she wrote a little post-it note saying she went for a run. The sun was just rising. Typical of New York City, there were already a good number of people rushing and bustling around. Derrick had his back to her. When he heard her approaching, he turned around and gave her a wry smile. He wore a tan suit and black dress shirt that were perfectly tailored. His blond hair was well combed and styled. Everything about him was just too perfect. By almost every woman's definition, he was hot. If it were not for the sinister look in his eyes, Rae might have been attracted to him. He scanned her figure from head to toe, as she walked up to him. She did not dress to impress, but wore an old pair of yoga pants and a red shirt. His gaze made her uncomfortable as usual, so she cleared her throat.

"Hello Raelynn," he glanced at his watch. "I'm glad for once you are on time."

Raelynn shrugged and didn't say anything. After a tense moment, he added, "So about last night…"

"Let's cut the chase, shall we? What do you want?" Rae interrupted.

"Ohhh? Always straight to the point huh, lil Miss Rae? That's one thing I like about you." He moved closer until his face was only a couple of inches from hers. She averted his eyes. He grabbed her chin with his thumb and forefinger and tilted her face upwards, so he could look into her eyes.

"We both know what I want. Do you want me to spell it out?"

Raelynn broke free of his hold and took a few steps back. Her heart sank, it was just what she thought, "He wanted to sleep with her."

"Why?" she asked sadly. "You can have any woman within fifty miles of New York City."

He simply chuckled. "What can I say? The heart wants what it wants."

When he didn't say anything else, Raelynn added, "Isn't there anything else I can give you?"

This time he laughed out loud. "What else could you possibly give me Raelynn that I don't have? Hmm? Nothing!!! I have all the money and influence I could possibly want. All I want is your beautiful body Rae."

Raelynn visibly looked like she was going to throw up, which only made him laugh.

"Why all the gloom and doom? Considering your secret, it is a very small price to pay. I won't even call it a price. Sleeping with me will be an experience you will never forget. In fact, I'm sure you'll come back on your own for more."

"And what if I don't agree?"

"Well you know what will happen, Baby girl. I'll casually let Madame Josephine know you are in a relationship with Bryan Okoye, a former target, if I may add." He took a few steps closer and gave her a pointed look. "You of all people know how Madame Josephine handles people who double-cross her."

Raelynn's eyes were now swimming with tears. She tried to appeal to his humane side, if it existed. "Please Derrick, I'm begging you. I'll do anything else. Just let me…"

"You got 24 hours to make a decision," he said cutting her off. "If I don't hear back from you then, I'll assume you didn't accept my proposition and I'll do what I have to do. Choose wisely." He turned on his heels and left.

Several hours later, Raelynn's phone rang. She was sitting on her bed a long time, staring into space. After her meeting with Derrick, she walked around aimlessly in a park. By the time she returned to her apartment, Bryan was long gone. He sent her a text which read, 'Happy anniversary Babe. Hope you are feeling much better today. Call me later.'

She glanced at the caller I.D. and saw it was one of her closest friends in the city, Bree. Bree sent several text messages earlier; none of which she read or responded to. She really didn't feel like picking up the call, but she knew Bree. If she didn't pick up now, Bree would hound her or come by her place to check up on her. She reluctantly picked up the phone and said, "Hello," a little groggily.

"Rae…girl I've been trying to reach you for hours. **Were** you sleeping? Where are you?"

"I'm at home."

"Are you sick? You sound a little under the weather."

Raelynn cleared her throat, "Um, yeah I suppose so."

"Do you want me to stop by later? Bring you some noodle soup from that Thai place we love?" Bree asked cheerily.

Raelynn cleared her throat again, "No, don't worry about it. I'm sure I just need a little rest."

"Ok Rae, you do that. Get some sleep. I'll stop by later to check up on you."

Before she could protest, Bree hung up. "Which was just like Bree," she thought with merriment. Bree always had the final say. She and Bree met three years ago at a modeling event and immediately clicked. Almost the same way she clicked with Bryan from their first meeting. Bree was real and down to earth, a sharp contrast to all the fake and superficial girls in their world. Bree was a talented fashion designer and Moreau Company offered her several contracts. Bree, however refused to work full time for them or anyone else for that matter. She liked being her own boss. Bree was one of the few people who knew she was married to Bryan. She was the only one who knew about her involvement with Madame Josephine. She was her confidant through and through. Raelynn trusted Bree with her own life. She wanted to tell her about the latest development with Derrick, but felt it appropriate to discuss with her in person. Her phone buzzed again; this time with an incoming Whatsapp call from Franck. Franck hardly ever called her, unless it was something serious.

"Something must be wrong," she thought and quickly picked up her phone again.

"Franck my man. What's up?"

The next thing Franck said drained blood from her face, and she thought she would pass out. After a few moments she hung up and continued to stare into space. "How much bad luck could one person get in a day," she wondered. She lay back on her bed and cried her heart out. A small part of her refused to believe what Franck just told her. In an instance, she came up with a course of action. She quickly looked at her call history and tapped on Bree's number. She couldn't carry out this plan on her own. She needed help.

Five

Bryan slowly opened his front door and walked into his loft, while yawing and stretching. It had been a long and tiring day at the office.

The loft looked particularly shiny today. He then remembered his cleaning lady came by today. Not that the place was ever a pigsty, for he was an extremely organized and clean guy. Some even said he was borderline obsessively compulsive (OCD). Whenever his cleaning lady came by, there wasn't much for her to do except polish and shine everything until it shinned bright like a diamond. He flopped down onto his comfortable grey leather sofa and dialed Rae. It went straight to voicemail, which was strange, because her phone usually had a full charge. Or maybe she was working on a project at work. She usually texted him beforehand if she was going to work late. He had not spoken to her all day, which also was peculiar. They always managed to text or call each other every few hours. Even if he got caught up in work and forgot to text her, she would always text him. He checked his messages again, nothing from her. Something was not right; he could feel it. "Please God, let her be alright," he prayed silently. He stood up and walked to his fridge. It was fully stocked. Until he met Rae, the fridge was usually empty, except for the left overs from the takeout food he bought from different restaurants. He rarely cooked. On the other hand, Rae loved cooking for him whenever she came by, even if she barely ate any of the food she made. He scanned the fridge, looked for a snack, and settled for some fish pie and a glass of banana-strawberry smoothie she made a few days ago.

After finishing the snack, he called her one more time. His call went to voicemail again. He gave up and walked into his bedroom to change his clothes. The first thing that caught his eye was a beautifully embroidered envelope with his name on it, laying on his California King mahogany bed. He immediately recognized the neat handwriting as Rae's. For some reason, he was filled with dread about opening it. Curiosity overcame this dread and he carefully opened the envelope and saw a letter. He sat by the edge of the bed to read it.

My Dear Bryan,

I'm so sorry. I wish I had the nerve to tell you this in person, but I don't. You have been the best husband and friend a girl could possibly ask for, and I have been less than honest with you. I'm not worthy of your love and affection.

I'm not the woman you think I am; at least not entirely. I made some grievous mistakes and alliances in the past which have come back to haunt me. I allowed someone to manipulate me into stealing from people for many years. The first time I met you, I was on a mission to steal something from you. But I couldn't bring myself to do it. It was I who tipped you about tightening your security after that. I could not let any of them hurt you. And now I am being blackmailed to have an affair with some guy in the company, because last night he found out we were married. I would rather die than cheat on you. But the person I work for is ruthless and if she finds out we are married, what she will do to me is worse than death. I decided to get away as far as I could from New York.

I am not the woman you think you married. My life is so messed up and I do not want you to have any share of that. You should not be tied by marriage to a criminal. I am providing you with a way out.

I wish I had more time to explain everything, but I really have to go. Thanks for everything.

I will always love you.

Raelynn.

P.S. Please stay away from the Moreau Company, I am begging you. Do not take this letter to the police or try to investigate anything. They have a network that runs really deep.

Bryan looked into the envelope and saw divorce papers she signed. His whole world came tumbling down. He sat for a few minutes in stunned silence. He reread the letter over and over again. His spiritual mentor, Jason had urged him to pray over his marriage. He had prayed if anything obstructed his marriage, be revealed. Now it had. God answered his prayers and a little part of him wished He had not answered them. Ignorance was indeed bliss. He dialed Jason's number and almost immediately, he picked up. After explaining in a few terse words what happened, Jason told him he was coming over and hung up. Bryan felt as though his heart had shattered into a thousand pieces. Clutching the letter to his chest in anguish, he slowly slid from the bed to the plush carpet beneath him. For the first time in his adult life, he broke down into tears and wept.

"Miss, are you sure you are okay?" another concerned stewardess asked Raelynn. She cried the entire flight. Despite how much she tried, she was unable to eat anything. Luckily she was in business class and could huddle into a blanket, cover her head with another one, and weep in peace until the stewardesses came back. She wished they would leave her alone.

She sniffed, wiped her nose, and answered in a gruff voice, "Yeah, thanks. I'll be fine."

"I'm so sorry for your loss, Miss. Please have some water. Douala is so hot. We wouldn't want you to pass out from dehydration."

"Are we landing soon?"

"Yeah, in about 40 minutes."

Raelynn nodded grimly and took the small bottle of water the stewardess held out. She managed to gulp down half the bottle before she went back under her blankets and continued to weep. There were two things she was crying for: Josh and her marriage. She could not believe it was possible for her to never see Josh again. She was flying back to Cameroon to confirm what Franck told her the day before. At least with Josh, there was some glimmer of hope. Until they found Josh's body, she would not believe he was gone forever.

On the other hand, there was no hope for her marriage. She burned it to the ground. She hated to serve him divorce papers when everything was going so well a couple of hours before. She hated she told him the truth about her career on paper and not in person. He deserved so much better. She knew it was a cowardly move. However, she could not find the nerve to look him in the face and tell him she was a thief. She could not bear it. She just couldn't. At least this way, the last memory of their time together was a pleasant one, and she would always hold on to that. Her mind went back to their second encounter. After that first meeting, she genuinely never thought she would see him again.

Two and a half years ago

Raelynn was smiling as she walked around the Harlem Meer Pond in Central Park. There was an adorable golden-brown Labrador puppy chasing a few butterflies at the edge of the pond. His owner was watching the puppy with merriment. The tall brunette guy looked up at her and smiled. She gave him a little wave and continued walking. It was not yet 10:00 am, but it was already getting very hot, which was typical for New York summers. She loved coming here every Sunday morning to stroll, relax, or read a book. She liked this particular corner of the park, because it was not as crowded as the other parts. She walked over to one of the trees, threw a blanket under the shade, and started to read. It was a detective novel from one of her favorite fiction writers, Jeffery Archer. The story was about a woman who was framed for the murder of her roommate and was now doing everything in her power to prove she was innocent and find out who actually committed the murder.

It started getting overwhelmingly hot, and after a couple of hours she walked over to the nearby Barnes and Noble bookstore. She went there almost every Sunday afternoon after her Central Park walk to either buy a book or just sit and read one of her books. She loved detective, fantasy, and mystery novels. She settled down by a window seat, with her feet tucked under her and continued reading her novel. She was reading a section in the novel where the heroine entered an isolated building with the murderer. He was about to confess all his crimes and then kill her. Her heart was beating faster than normal in anticipation. Just then someone tapped her on the shoulder. She jumped in her seat frightened and shrieked.

"Raelynn?" a familiar voice asked. "I'm so sorry. I didn't mean to scare you."

She turned and looked up and her eyes met with Bryan's, who was looking at her with a wry smile and amusement in his eyes. He was wearing a wine-colored polo shirt and black khaki shorts with tan sneakers. He looked as dashing as she remembered.

"Bryan?" she replied in surprise and put a hand over her chest in relief. "No, I'm sorry. I just didn't see you there."

She stood up and greeted him with a warm hug; which lasted longer than it should have. After they pulled apart, he asked, "How have you been? It's been a while." It was three months to be exact. Similar to the first time he saw her, she took his breath away. She was simple, but fashionably dressed in a cute orange sundress with a small sleeveless denim jacket and white wedges. Similar to the first time they met, she had on a black and brown curly weave, which fell down the middle of her back. Although she was not wearing as much makeup as she had on the boat, she looked stunning. In fact, he thought, "She looks better with less makeup on."

"I'm good. How are you?" she asked and motioned him to sit across from her. "Care to join me?"

"Of course," he answered smiling and sat down. "Sorry to interrupt. What were you reading?"

"Oh," she said showing him a cover of the book. "Just a little detective book."

"Jeffery Archer?" he asked leaning in to read the title. "He's one of the best. I used to love reading his books in college."

"Yeah. He's awesome. You don't read his books anymore?"

"Nahh, not really. Life caught up with me, I guess. I'm too busy for that these days."

"Oh yeah. I can't imagine how busy it is to be the manager of a million-dollar company."

Bryan chuckled softly, leaned back in his chair and studied her. For a moment, they just sat staring at each other.

"What are you doing here by the way?" she finally asked. "If I remember correctly, you live in Long Island."

"Can't a brother just hang out in a bookstore?" he said smiling. He didn't want to tell her he hired someone to find her. He got her address a few weeks ago, but did not want to seem creepy by just walking up to her doorstep. So he found out her popular spots and came by the bookstore purposely to see her.

"Ummmm," Rae replied, tilting her head to the side a little and giving him a suspicious look.

"You just said you don't have much time to read."

He shrugged, "Alright, alright. You got me. Truth is…" He leaned forward and rested his elbows on his knee and said honestly, "I know you come here sometimes. I was hoping to run into you."

Raelynn was visibly taken aback. The man went out of his way to find her after all these weeks. It was really sweet and creepy at the same time. If she had not done her own background check on him before they met, she would have been a little freaked out. If she dared to admit it to herself, she thought about him often since they met. She even stalked him on social media a bit after the boat party. The Nigerian tabloids were constantly talking about him. It was rumored that he was dating some actress from Nollywood. When she read that piece of gossip, she felt as if her blood would boil. She knew it was ridiculous for her to feel that way, because she had no stake on the guy. They only met once and she was sure they would never meet again. Still, jealousy knows no rationale, and she pouted for days.

"How did you know I would be here?" she asked softly.

"Don't worry about it," he replied leaning back into his chair. "I have my ways."

Sweet as he was, she did not want to get involved with him in any way. He seemed like a really good guy and with her life being as messed up as it was, she would bring him nothing but trouble. She took a deep breath and started, "It's so sweet that you went to all that trouble. But Bryan…."

"Hold on a sec," he interrupted holding his hand up. "I know you said your life is complicated. But you seem like a really nice person and I was simply hoping we could be friends. Surely your life isn't too complicated for a friendship."

She sighed and gave him a long-leveled look before replying. "Well when you put it that way… Just friends?" He nodded and she smiled broadly. "In that case, I'll be more than happy to oblige."

They continued chatting enthusiastically until the store closed and they had to leave. He coaxed her into having dinner with him. They went to one of her favorite Thai restaurants. After dinner, they walked along 5th Avenue to window-shop. She bought a very fashionable hat from one of the stores. When it became late, she said goodbye so she could catch a cab back to New Jersey. Bryan however insisted on seeing her home and called his driver to give them a ride. He had the latest Tesla car, which is a top car in the industry. As they rode in his fancy vehicle, they started talking about politics in Cameroon.

"So you mean to tell me that one guy was president for over 40 years?" Bryan asked astonished.

"Yup. The guy refused to leave office."

"That's insane. How come the people have not risen against him and kicked him out?"

"Pssffft," Raelynn said waving her hand in dismissal. "Cameroonians are the most compliant people I know, especially the Francophones. They would rather die in poverty and marginalization than to stand up against anything."

Bryan shook his head slowly. "In Naija, we wouldn't stand for that kind of nonsense. How did he manage to stay in power so long? He seemed really old."

Raelynn then proceed to tell him all the diabolical things the former Cameroonian president had done to maintain power.

They soon reached her apartment and Bryan slowly walked her to the door.

"Alright, here we are. Goodnight. I had such a wonderful day."

"The pleasure was all mine, Raelynn. Goodnight. I'll hit you up later." He gave her a heartfelt hug and waited until she entered her apartment before walking back to his car.

They continued to be just friends for over six months. They found themselves talking or texting on the phone every day for hours. They met every Sunday morning for brunch and a walk, when the weather permitted. They developed strong feelings for each other and Bryan eventually asked her to be his girlfriend. Although she knew it might lead to disaster later on for the both of them, she agreed and they started dating.

***

The Douala Airport was congested with hundreds of people. Several airlines including Brussels and Air France landed within the hour. The carousels were crowded and it took Raelynn over an hour to get her luggage. When she finally stepped out of the airport, she was bombarded with a wave of heat. She never understood how people lived in this kind of city. It was so hot; the heat felt like something was weighing her down. Several young men came up to her and offered to carry her bags. She ignored them. You can never trust anyone in Douala airports. Some of her friends lost their bags because someone offered to help carry them and then disappeared with them. Nevertheless, one overzealous guy picked up one of her bags. She took off her dark sunshades and gave him one of her model glares, which was enough to make a giant quiver. He immediately dropped the bag and went off to find somebody else. She put on her shades again and continued walking. As she walked towards the parking lot, she saw Franck and waved. He waved back at her and walked towards her. He wore a simple pair of tan shorts and a white T-shirt. Two of her cousins, Lum and Tita accompanied him.

Something tugged at his heart as Franck walked towards her. She looked fashionable as always in black ripped jeans, with an off-the-shoulder dark grey blouse and brown mid-calf high-heeled boots. In spite of the big sunglasses she wore, her face was withdrawn and tired. He suspected his face looked the exact same way. When he heard news of Josh, he shed a few bitter tears. This was the first time in his adult life he cried. Josh was one of his closest friends ever since they were children, running around the village causing havoc. Although there was some hope Josh was still alive, he secretly believed Josh was dead. When he caught up with Raelynn, he gave her an affectionate hug.

After exchanging greetings, she immediately jumped to the matter occupying their thoughts. "So, on the phone you said you found Josh's blood all over Laura's apartment in Buea?"

Laura was Josh's current girlfriend. She and Raelynn did not exactly get along. Well, to be honest, most of the animosity came from Raelynn. Raelynn sent most of the money she earned from Madame Josephine to Josh and she suspected Laura was only with Josh because of his money. Sure she claimed she was a Christian, but Raelynn felt she used it as a cover to swindle her twin brother.

Franck cleared his throat, "Yeah. From what she told us, he left Douala and went to Buea to spend the weekend with her. She was gone Saturday night for some retreat at her church. When she came home the next morning, he was no where to be found and there was blood all over her living room."

"Are we sure it's Josh's blood?" Raelynn probed.

"We had the police match it with his medical records," Lum answered. "So many things have changed since you left, Sis." Things definitely had changed. "It's a new procedure for Cameroonian hospitals to keep blood records of their patients."

Raelynn nodded grimly, "It's been two days, Have the police been able to find anything?"

"Sadly no," Franck said shaking his head. "They said they're still looking. I even gave them a huge incentive to motivate them with their search. They still got nothing. We just have to be patient."

"I don't want to be patient," Raelynn snapped. "My brother could be lying somewhere dying. We have to find him before anything worse happens to him."

Turning to Tita, she added, *"Aseh eh Tita, you know that Laura ei house for Buea?"*

"Yeah, I know am(it)." Tita responded.

"We fi go there?"

"Now, now so?" Tita asked in surprise. *"You no go rest first?"*

Raelynn shook her head. *"Buea no far nor. No bi only 30 minutes. Make we di go. Call ei sey we di come."* And with that, the others helped her carry her luggage to Tita's Rav4 and they started out for Buea.

Six

Due to heavy traffic in Bonaberi, the neighborhood that leads into Douala, it took over two hours for them to get to Laura's place. Tita parked in front of the small pink colored house and dialed Laura's number. She answered on the third ring and said she would meet them outside in a minute. As they stood outside waiting for her, Raelynn took a good look at the surroundings. The house was newly built and fairly isolated from the other houses down the road. This would explain why no one in the neighborhood saw or heard anything that fateful Saturday night. Compared to most of the other towns in Cameroon, Buea did not have any dust, which made the air clean and easier to breathe. Furthermore, the weather was relatively cool and one could have mistaken the town for a small city in a temperate zone.

Laura came out from the back door to meet them. She was a petite lady, not more than 5 feet tall.

She was simply dressed in a plain old black skirt and a sky-blue blouse. Even her hair was simple, no weaves, braids, or anything. It was her natural hair, which was tied up in a simple knot at the back of her head. Her eyes looked a little red and puffy, as though she was crying. She had a pretty face though, Raelynn had to give her that. "She looks like the house help," Raelynn thought. She wondered what Josh saw in her. She was not like the girls or women he typically chased after; women with style and class. He sent her a bunch of pictures of the girls that he dated before, and they were all exquisite beauties and superbly dressed, with their hair and nails impeccably done. They looked good enough to compete with her, an American model. Well, there must be something else about this Laura girl that none of the other girls had.

Laura walked up to them and greeted each of them with a hug. It got a little awkward when she reached for Raelynn, with both of them mumbling greetings.

"Welcome to my place. Please come on in," Laura said and motioned for them to follow her. To their surprise, she skipped past the front door and led them in through the back door.

"I apologize for taking you in this way," she explained on her way. "I've not been able to go through the living room since…you know."

"Josh's blood was found all over your living room?" Raelynn asked bluntly.

Her companions turned and gaped at her. It was not like her to be so blunt. She ignored them.

"Yeah." Laura responded weakly.

"I'd like to see it," Raelynn added. "If you don't mind."

Laura nodded weakly and replied, "Sure." Laura led the way to the living room but refused to go in. Raelynn and the others walked right in and looked around. The place was properly scrubbed down and there was no sign of blood anywhere in the room. Raelynn sensed a bad omen in the room.

She took her time, staring at every single object in that room. It was almost as if she was willing for them to talk--to tell her exactly what happened here on Saturday. Franck, Tita, and Lum eventually left her alone as she continued to study the room. There was not much to see. It was a basic living room with a small table and four chairs, a cupboard and one brown couch. Nonetheless, Raelynn was there for almost an hour.

When she left the living room, she found the rest of her companions in the kitchen eating a Cameroonian delicacy, ekwang. It was made from ground cocoyam wrapped up in cocoyam leaves and mixed with fried tomatoes, fish, and meat. It was one of Raelynn's favorite meals. Right now, she still had no appetite for food. As they were eating, she continued probing Laura with all kinds of questions.

"So you said, you left the apartment at 8:00 pm for something at church?"

"Yeah."

"You said you hadn't seen Josh in a while. When he comes to visit you, you decide to spend all night in church? Did you guys get into a fight or something?"

"Oh no, not at all. Josh knows our relationship comes second to our relationship with God. He was actually planning on coming to the Revival retreat. He just wasn't feeling particularly well that morning."

Raelynn rolled her eyes. Here we go again with this Christian nonsense. She believed there was some "higher power" out there. But how could a relationship with your partner come in second to your relationship with a guy who is invisible? That was just crazy. Besides, what did she mean he was planning to go to church with her?

"Sorry, you said Josh was planning to go to church with you? Why?"

"Umm," she stuttered a little. "Because he wanted to. Ever since he gave his life to Christ, we've gone to a couple of church functions together."

Wait. What? Raelynn was taken aback. Josh was a Christian? When? He was the one who claimed science-disproved religion. He only believed in things one could see, hear, and touch. In his opinion, anything Christians called miracles or what some cultures called a taboo, were just circumstances science had not yet explained. He liked using twins as an example. Before people understood reproduction, Christians saw twins as a miracle and some cultures saw twins as taboo. But with science, it was easily explained that identical twins are from a fertilized egg, which split up early in development, and fraternal twins are from two different fertilized eggs.

How could the same person who used science to argue so passionately against Christianity, now be a Christian himself? Raelynn shook her head and thought to herself. "None of this made any sense." She decided to file this thought away for later.

"He wasn't feeling well before you left, huh? What was wrong with him?"

"Just a little cold. Headache, sore throat…you know. I gave him some painkillers and told him to get some rest. When I returned home, I saw…" Laura broke off in a sob and covered her mouth with her hand.

Raelynn nodded grimly and turned away. Tears were brimming at the back of her eyes. She barely held herself together. She had to stay strong for Josh.

"When you guys talked in the weeks before, did he mention any problems or disagreements he had with anyone?"

Laura shook her head and sniffled. "No, everything seemed fine. He wasn't communicating as much, because in the village he and Anthony were visiting, Boko Haram had destroyed all the communication lines."

"Hmmmmm," was Raelynn's reply. "You didn't leave the church at any time for any reason?"

"No, I was there the entire time. I was…" Laura broke off again and gave Raelynn a skeptical look, as she understood what Raelynn was getting at. "What are you trying to say? You think I had something to do with Josh's attack?"

Franck, Tita, and Lum finished eating and were watching them. Lum stood up and held out her hands as a sign of surrender.

"Laura, please. I'm sure that's not what Rae meant."

Raelynn huffed. "No of course not. It's just that...well, you are his girlfriend and also the last person to see him before he vanished. Plus, we found his blood all over your living room. Maybe you guys got into some kind of fight and in a moment of passion, someone got hurt..." Raelynn mimicked Lum and also put up her hands. "I'm just saying."

Laura looked like she was about to boil up in anger. She took a few deep breaths to calm herself before responding, "If you must know, I love Josh very much, and I would never hurt him in any way. Could you please leave? I would really appreciate it. I will not stand here in my own house and have someone accuse me of assault or murder."

"Fine, I'll leave. But know this, the truth about my brother will be uncovered soon. I swear to you if I find out you had anything to do with his disappearance, I will personally make sure you regret it." Raelynn turned on her heels and strode off out of the house.

Franck, Lum, and Tita stayed behind to apologize to Laura for Raelynn's behavior. When they all got back to the car, Tita demanded in pidgin, *"Asehhh ehhh, na weti di worry you eh Raelynn?"*

Raelynn turned to look at him with a thunderous gaze. *"Weti di worry me?"* she asked, her voice rising. "My brother has been missing for two days. He could be out there severely injured or even dead. You have the effrontery to ask, *'Na weti di worry me?'* " The emotions she had bottled up for two days came to surface and she could not seem to control them.

"Rae, please calm down." Lum pleaded.

"Why should I calm down?"

"Look Rae," Franck said calmly. "I know you are frustrated. We all are. But getting pissed off and throwing out accusations at people isn't going to solve anything. You don't have any concrete evidence. You're only going to make things worse. We might need her help to solve this case."

Raelynn leaned back in her chair. She knew he was right. Her attack on Laura was uncalled for. She was the last person who saw her brother and her apartment might be the only clue they had to solving his disappearance. Maybe deep down, Laura was in as much pain as Rae was. It would not be wise to make enemies with the woman.

After a few moments, Raelynn said somberly. "You are right Franck. I know I'm being a pain in the butt. I'm sorry guys. I should apologize."

"It's ok." The rest of the crew mumbled. "We cannot imagine what you are going through."

Raelynn stepped out of the car again and walked back to the house. She got into the house via the backdoor and found Laura in the kitchen washing dishes while dashing tears from her eyes. When she heard Raelynn's entry, she looked up at her apprehensively.

"Look," Raelynn said putting up her hands in surrender. "I came back to say I'm sorry. I had no reason to attack you like that."

Laura's gaze softened. "It's all good. I'm sorry too, for kicking you out. You have every right to be frustrated and angry right now."

Raelynn nodded grimly, fighting back tears. One escaped from her right eye, and she brushed it away furiously.

"Yeah, I just hope that he is ok, wherever he is."

"I pray so."

Raelynn cleared her throat. "I should get going," she said walking to the door.

"Yeah. Please let me know if you find anything else," Laura tossed back.

When Raelynn got back to the car, Tita drove them to Josh's apartment in the capital of Cameroon Yaoundé, which was a four-hour drive. Bundled up with each of their own emotions, they barely spoke throughout the journey.

The sun was setting when Tita pulled up to Josh's house in Etude, an upscale neighborhood in Yaoundé. It was a striking cream-colored bungalow with a lavish garden surrounding it. There were two other cars parked outside, a Mercedes Benz sports car and a Hummer Jeep. Unlike his twin, Josh went to college. He graduated as a chemical engineer from one of the private American universities about a year ago with honors. In addition to his knack for science, he had keen business acumen. With all the money Raelynn sent him, he started up a cement business in Yaoundé, which was thriving. His company was rivaling with the top cement companies in the region.

He lived with two of his cousins, Lum and Kingsley, as well as a housekeeper, Agnes, and a driver, John. There was a young man standing on the balcony, who waved at them as they got out of the car. He looked a couple of years older than she was, about twenty-eight years old, give or take. He had to be Anthony. She recognized him from the Whatsapp pictures Josh sent a couple of months ago. He was as fine as he looked in the pictures. His skin was very fair, almost like the color of sand. He had an athletic build, with no trace of fat. He did not have too much muscle either. He was about six feet tall. He walked up to them and extended a hand to Raelynn.

"Hi. You must be the infamous Raelynn. I'm Anthony. I've heard so much about you. It's unfortunate we had to meet under these circumstances. We are going to…"

His voice was drifting off, as Raelynn lost consciousness. She hadn't eaten in almost two days and she was weak. She felt drowsy in the car, but she fought it off. Right now, she could not fight it any longer. Her hand slowly slipped from his, as her feet gave way and everything went black. The last thing she remembered was someone yelling, "Rae! Rae! Wake up."

Raelynn slowly opened her eyes and blinked. She was lying on a comfortable bed, staring up at a white ceiling. She blinked again. Where was she? She tried to sit up, but she felt strong hands pushing her shoulders back onto the bed. She heard a voice say,

"Don't get up just yet. You need to rest."

She obliged and lay back down. She turned her head a little to the right and gazed up at Anthony who was sitting on a chair. His eyes were dancing with amusement as he gazed down at her and smiled. Oh wow. He had such a dazzling smile. Not that she should be thinking about things like that now.

"What happened?" she asked woozily and cleared her throat.

"You fainted," he responded. "How are you feeling?"

"A little weak. I'm sure I'll be fine."

"You gave us a scare there for a minute? What is the last thing you remember?"

"You were introducing yourself and then…that's it. That's all I remember. Everything went black." She put a hand to her head and groaned, remembering how undernourished her body was. She was also severely dehydrated.

"I'm sorry about that. I'm just a little dehydrated, I think."

"And here I thought you just took one good look at my face and passed out," he chuckled. "I'm kidding. Lum did one quick examination and said you were probably just dehydrated. We forced some sugar water down your throat. I can see she was right. Her nursing classes are really starting to pay off."

Raelynn nodded curtly. She was beginning to feel a little uncomfortable. She was lying down on a bed, and alone in a room with a guy she barely knew. It did not matter that he was so hot. Not that she cared. She was still very much in love with Bryan.

Anthony seemed to read her thoughts and jumped to his feet.

"Oh, I'm sorry. This must seem so weird. Waking up in a strange room with a guy you just met. Lemme call the others. They left about a minute before you woke up." With that, he swiftly left the room and shut the door behind him.

Raelynn closed her eyes again and tried to get a little rest. It seemed she barely closed her eyes, when she heard a knock. She asked them to come in. Franck, Tita, and Lum all filed in, along with the house-help, Agnes on their heels, carrying a tray of food. It was one of her favorite meals, dodo (sliced fried plantains) and ndole (sweet bitter leaf and groundnut soup) with foot-cow. Although she still had no appetite, she forced a couple of bites down her throat. She had to keep her strength up. Her falling sick was not going to help Josh in any way. Franck, Tita, and Lum regaled her with stories from their childhood, while she ate.

Franck narrated a story of Rae, Josh, Lum and him playing hide-and-seek when they were about seven years old. Josh hid under a couch and had fallen asleep for hours. The rest of them spent the entire afternoon looking for him. Rae eventually had to report to their mother Josh was missing. Her mom alerted all the neighbors and they began frantically searching for him, only for one of them to find him napping under the couch. Rae chuckled when she remembered how relieved and then outraged her mom was. She spanked him so hard he could not sit properly for three days.

They left her alone to rest after she finished eating. Within moments, she fell into a deep, dreamless sleep.

She blinked against the bright morning sun and quickly sat up in bed. She was a little disoriented. Where was she? How long had she been asleep? She gently rubbed her temples with her fingers, as she tried to remember. Oh, yes. She remembered she was in Yaoundé, in one of Josh's rooms. She also remembered having dinner here with Franck, Tita, and Lum. She must have fallen asleep after that. She groaned, as she swung her legs to the floor and walked to the adjoining bathroom to relieve herself. She groaned again after taking one good look at herself in the mirror. She looked ghastly. Her long black weave, which typically had every hair in place, was now pointing in every direction. Her face looked tired and withdrawn. Her eyes looked a little blood-shot, as though she had been drinking for hours. She blew on her hand to get a waft of her breath and urghhh it smelled terrible. She had not showered in two days and she could almost see the wriggly lines of smell emanating from her body.

First order of business, she immediately brushed her teeth, showered and spent a great deal of time fixing her hair. When she was done, she put on a simple dark blue romper. She applied light makeup, after she had dressed up. Ahhh, she felt human again. A shower could do wonders to someone's psyche. She felt rejuvenated and alive; ready to continue her quest to find Josh. She slipped on some white sandals and left the room. Since she had been unconscious when she first came into the house, she now took her time exploring the place, as she made her way to where she thought the living room would be. Seeing no one there, she made her way to the balcony and saw Anthony there again.

He was leaning against the railing and staring into the yard in deep contemplation. He had his back towards her and even from behind, his physique was amazing. He had well-padded muscles on his upper back, which tapered down to his waist. Not that she cared. She liked to appreciate a fine man when she saw one. She must have made a noise, because he suddenly turned around and caught her studying him. His eyes lit up at the sight of her and he smiled.

"Heyyy, good morning Rae. How are you feeling today?"

"I'm feeling a lot better Anthony. Thanks for asking."

"Please call me Tony," he answered flashing another radiant smile. "I can see you are doing a lot better. You look amazing."

Raelynn smiled coyly. "Thanks. I was a mess yesterday. Franck told me you were the one who carried me upstairs after I passed out. Thanks for doing that."

"It was nothing," he responded dismissively. "You weigh practically nothing."

She smiled again and walked up to the balcony rail and leaned her elbows on it.

"So what brings you here so early this morning, Tony?"

"It's not that early my dear. It's 11:00 am. I just came by to check in on you and see how you were doing."

"Awww really? Thanks. That's very kind of you."

"Trust me my Dear. It was my pleasure."

They stood side-by-side for a few moments in silence, gazing into the bright green courtyard.

Suddenly, she turned to face him and asked in a voice that was barely a whisper.

"When was the last time you saw Josh?"

Tony turned around and leaned his back against the rail before he answered pensively. "The last time I saw Josh was last Friday. We went to Bibemi in the North region a month ago to sell some of our products. You see, most of the buildings in the town had been destroyed by a Boko Haram raid months ago. Hence, the town was in great need of reconstruction and needed a ton of cement. We went there to help and make some money. Unfortunately, while we were there, there was another Boko Haram raid. They cut off the entire communication network in the town. We laid low for a while." He took in a deep breath before continuing. "Earlier last week, things settled down and we decided to leave. We got to Garoua on Wednesday and booked a flight to Douala on Thursday. We took care of some business in Douala both Thursday and Friday. We were supposed to leave Douala for Yaoundé Friday evening, but he said he wanted to stop by Buea and see Laura, since it wasn't too far, before heading back to Yaoundé. I dropped him off in Buea before heading to Douala. That was the last time I saw him."

Raelynn watched him intently the entire time he spoke. When he was done, there was another brief pause before she asked, "You spent more time with him than anyone. Do you know anyone who might want to hurt him? Anyone he had a beef with?"

Tony shook his head, "No I can't imagine who would want to hurt him. He was the most amicable person I've ever met. Everyone loves him. Both the clients and the workers think very highly of him. Why anyone would attack him is beyond me. It really breaks my heart to hear what happened."

She nodded briefly. He was right. Everyone did indeed love Josh. He had such a way with people. Making even the most reserved person laugh and feel at ease. She envied him a little for having such social grace.

"And besides," Tony went on. "Since he became a Christian, he has been extra generous and kind. I didn't think it were possible, but people loved him more than they did before."

"So it was really true that he was a Christian, huh?" Raelynn thought.

"When did he become a Christian?" she asked.

"Ummmm, well...let me see," Tony said as he stared up at the ceiling in reflection. "I think it was about six months ago. From what he told me, Mr. Oben, one of our clients invited him to church for Easter. Something happened to him during that service and he told me his life was transformed. I didn't quite understand his decision. I've known him for three years and he was a staunch atheist."

"I know right?" Raelynn agreed. "I've never known anyone else so vehemently opposed to religion in any form. And then one service completely changes his mind? It must have been one heck of a sermon."

"You know what?" Tony said leaning in closer as if he were telling her a secret. "I know this might sound a little crazy, but I have a feeling that church might have bewitched him."

Raelynn narrowed her eyes, "Hmmm. I didn't think about that. But now that you mention it, it might be true. Before I left Paye, there were all these churches that were rumored to actually be cults. Maybe the church he attended was one of them."

"Right? Right?" he gave her a little grin. "Thank goodness you feel the same way. I thought I was a little crazy."

She smiled back at him and said nothing.

"Hey look," he said putting a comforting hand on her arm. "I'm sure Josh will be fine. He is a very resilient guy. He'll show up soon."

"Thanks Tony. I hope so too."

"I'll do anything I can to help you find him. All you gotta do is ask, ok?"

Raelynn nodded again, fighting back tears in the back of her eyes. "Josh was like a brother to me. I'll make sure we find him, ok?"

"Yeah, thanks again Tony."

"No problem. We'll find him. But in the meantime, if you want to take a look at the facilities of the company, I'd be happy to show you around. At the risk of sounding proud, I must say, we are very pleased with our company."

"That would be great Tony. I'd love to."

"It will be fine," he said reassuringly. Before she knew what was happening, he reached out and pulled her into his arms in a big bear hug. She wrapped her own arms around his waist and hugged him back. When they pulled apart, he said, "I have to go down to the store and attend to a few things. Take care of you. I'll see you later, ok?"

She simply nodded and watched, as he walked to his black Prado parked in front of the house.

Raelynn waved back at Tony, as he maneuvered his car onto the main street and drove off. She stood there for a moment thinking about Josh. She closed her eyes as she remembered one particular instance when they were ten years old, two years before their mother passed away.

***

One of their mom's boyfriends came up to her, while Raelynn was in the kitchen doing the dishes. Her mother stepped out to go to the store and Josh was playing football with some of his mates.

"Hmmm, Baby Rae, you are developing into a woman, eh?" the fellow said and ogled her chest. He was a chubby man in his forties with round cheeks and a protruding belly. Raelynn felt distinctly uncomfortable and did not know how to respond.

"You should come over to my place later," he continued. "I have many nice things for a pretty girl like you."

"No thank you Sir, I'm good."

"You mean you don't like nice things?"

"My mother gives me all the nice things I need, Sir."

"Oh really, does she? I am the one who gives her all those nice things. I have a lot more than she does.

You think I'm playing? Here, see." He said and pulled out a couple of 10,000 CFA bills and flashed them at her. "See, I can give you all of this. You just have to touch me in a very special place."

Raelynn felt nauseous and vehemently shook her head. Without warning, the fellow grabbed her hand and started pulling her hand towards his special place. "C'mon child. Stop pretending you don't like nice things. Just touch me here now."

Raelynn shrieked as she tried to pull her hand away. Just then, Josh walked into the kitchen and saw them. A rage, she had never seen before overcame him. He picked up a plate and threw it at the fellow's face. The fellow dodged just in time and the plate fell with a crash on the floor. Josh then grabbed a knife from the counter and pointed at the fellow. "Step away from my sister," he yelled. Raelynn escaped to a far end of the kitchen.

"Hey, hey, hey," the fellow said, putting his hands up. "What is your problem boy? We were just talking."

"I don't care. Get out of my house," Josh replied.

The fellow laughed. "Your house? Please. Look at the twat, trying to threaten me. Do you know who I am?"

"I don't care who you are. Leave, now and never come back."

When the guy made no move to leave. Josh picked up another plate and threw it at him. The fellow dodged again, walked up, and smoothly grabbed the knife out of Josh's hand. "Small boy, don't play games with me, ehh," the fellow said. "I can destroy you." Instead of being intimidated, Josh kicked the fellow squarely on his crotch and gave him a solid blow on his nose, which almost broke it. As the fellow was still bent over from the blow, Josh reached for a frying pan Raelynn had just washed and hit the fellow squarely on the head with it.

"Now get out of my house," he repeated. The fellow looked at him with murder in his eyes and then walked out the door saying, "You and your stupid mother will regret this."

Josh rushed to Raelynn's side and held her hand. "Are you okay? Did that man hurt you?"

"No, I'm fine. Thanks Josh. I was really scared though. It's a good thing you came in."

"Rae, you gotta learn how to fight back and defend yourself. I may not always be around to help you."

"Yeah, you are right. Could you teach me?"

"Of course Sis. I'll teach you."

They reported the incident to their mom when she came back home and she broke things off with the guy. Over the next few days, Josh taught Raelynn a couple of self-defense techniques he learned from some of his older friends: the low blow, eye gouging, a strong punch and knee into the groin. The techniques came in handy over the next upcoming years.

Their mother was a promiscuous woman. She was not even sure who was Raelynn and Josh's father. She got pregnant with them after a drunken one-night stand. Her family stopped communicating with her, because of her lifestyle. Raelynn and Josh's peers constantly humiliated and made fun of them, because of their mother. So from a very young age, Raelynn and Josh grew up learning how to depend upon and trust only each other. As they were growing up, there was a constant tirade of their mom's boyfriends in and out of their house. On a few occasions, some of them made inappropriate advances to her as a child, but fortunate for her, Josh was always by her side, which made it easier for the two of them to scare the fellows off.

Their mother's promiscuity eventually gave her HIV. The virus killed her, when Raelynn and Josh were twelve. After her mother's funeral, Raelynn vowed to never sleep with a guy until they were married. Looking at her mother's life, she did not want to be a single mother like her mom or contract some STD or AIDS by having premarital sex…

***

A deep cough broke her away from her reverie. She turned and saw Franck standing behind her.

"Good morning Rae." He smiled and gave her a hug. "How did you sleep?"

"Good morning Franck," she replied warmly. "I slept surprisingly well. I feel rejuvenated. How are ya?"

"Yeah, you look like it. *I'm aite*. Wanna join me for breakfast?"

"Sure. Isn't it a little too late for that though?" she chuckled.

"Ha. You Americans. Call it brunch if you must. Breakfast is simply the first meal of the day in my opinion."

He entered the house and led the way to the dining table. It was made from carved red oak wood; a simple but elegant set. On the table, lay enough food for a small party. There were pancakes, scrambled eggs, toasted bread, chocolate, dodo (sliced fried plantains), tea, hot chocolate, puff-puff and pap. All of the food looked yummy.

"Oh my goodness," Raelynn cried as she sat down. "Who's all this food for? I'm full just by looking at it."

"Mm mm. Don't start talking like that. This food is all for you ooo. I didn't know what you wanted for breakfast, so I asked Agnes to cook up a variety of things. You can choose whatever you want."

"Wow! That is so sweet. And I know what I want." She reached for a puff-puff and plopped it into her mouth. "Mmmmmm, this is so good. I haven't had this in ages."

"I bet. You models." He shook his head. "You are as thin as a rail."

Raelynn laughed as she grabbed another puff-puff and poured some pap into a bowl. Franck put some dodo and eggs onto his plate. While they were eating, Raelynn asked, "So, have you heard anything from the detective looking into Josh's case? What's his name?"

"Detective Harrison Asanga. I called him this morning. Still no news," Anthony answered grimly.

Raelynn's shoulders dropped in disappointment. The longer it took for them to find him, the more likely it was that they would find a corpse. She pushed her unfinished plate of food away; having lost her appetite again.

"Could you please give me his number? I'd like to talk to him in person."

"Yeah sure."

"I want to hire my own search party, if that's possible. I'm sure you can easily find some guys who are willing to help. Money won't be a problem. I'll pay them whatever they want."

Franck paused to chew and swallow the food in his mouth before replying, "I already hired a search party. Still no news from them either."

"How many guys do you have now?"

"Three."

"Make it ten. And don't limit the search to Buea. They should look in Limbe, Douala, etc. In fact, all of Cameroon, if necessary."

Franck simply nodded. A brief silence followed before he asked calmly,

"When are you going to tell Ma Bridget?"

Raelynn buried her hands in her face. How could she possibly break this kind of news to Ma Bridget? But she knew she had to find a way to break this news to her grand-aunt, the woman who loved her like a daughter and taken care of she and Josh after their mother died. She was old and frail now. The news would probably send her to her grave.

"I'll give it sometime. By some miracle, Josh may show up. I don't want to give her a heartache for no reason."

Franck tilted his head a little to the side and considered.

"But what if something has happened to him? She's not going to be happy knowing we kept her in the dark."

"I'll take my chances," Raelynn said and leaned back in her chair. "I miss him, Franck."

"I know. I do too," he said solemnly and reached out to grab her hand in comfort.

"What if something has happened to him? What if I never see him again?" Against her will, a tear slipped down from her right eye and she cried.

"Hey, hey," Franck said standing up. He came and stood behind her chair, wrapped his arms around her shoulders and leaned down to rest his head on hers. "You can't think like that. You gotta stay positive. We'll find him."

Raelynn reached out and gently patted his arms. "I hope we will. I really hope we will."

Seven

Raelynn gasped, as one obnoxious motorcycle driver cut off her driver on the highway. She was in constant fear that one day they would be involved in a serious automobile accident. Driving in Cameroon was a nightmare. Not only did you have to deal with other drivers, you also had to deal with cattle on the road and motorcycle riders who did not obey the law. It was not uncommon for a taxi-driver to stop in the middle of the street to pick up or drop off a passenger, regardless of who was behind him. The motorcycle riders were the worst; they frequently cut people without any warning.

Tony tried to teach her to drive, but after doing one practice run on the main street, she pulled over to the curb and never got behind the wheel again. She was more than happy to let the driver, John, drive her everywhere. John was a tall, lanky, middle-aged man with dark chocolate skin complexion. He worked with Josh for over two years and was totally devoted to him. He extended his devotion to Josh's twin sister, Raelynn. Over the past few weeks, Raelynn and John became good friends. They shared individual stories about Josh and bonded over their mutual loss of a brother and employer. It had been three weeks since she came to Cameroon and there was no sign of him anywhere. Though a part of her hoped he was alive somewhere, deep down she knew he was no more. She just had to get closure now. She cried to sleep almost every night and sometimes even randomly burst into tears during the day. She was so fortunate to have so many friends and family to comfort her during this trying season. Lum and Tita were good about keeping her company and distracting her these past few weeks. Franck also was a champ. Though he lived 30 minutes from the house, he drove over every other day to check on her. When he did not come over, he never failed to call her to make sure she was okay.

However, the real MVP was Tony. She spent most of her time at the company with him, going over figures and getting a tour of the facility. When she did not come to the store, Anthony would stop by the family house after work. He always insisted they go out into the city and have some fun. They visited all the hot spots in the city: the mall, the museums, a few amusement parks, the best restaurants in the city, the theater, Jardin du Plaisir in downtown Yaoundé, etc. This helped her get her mind off Josh for at least a couple of hours. Tony was a cool, funny, and attractive guy to hang out with. If she wasn't still in love with Bryan, she could fall in love with Tony. But

Bryan was still her one and only true love. It will take a while for that to change, if ever. When she was not thinking about Josh, she was thinking about Bryan. She wondered what he was doing, how he reacted after reading her letter, if he had moved on, was he thinking about her as much as she was thinking about him? She desperately wanted to call him, but she refrained. Madame Josephine and her minions were probably watching him, maybe even taping his calls in hopes of finding out where she was. She would not make that fatal error of calling Bryan. No matter how badly she wanted to reach out to him, she had to be strong, for his safety as well as hers. She thought with fondness, about the day he had proposed.

About eighteen months ago

It was a cool spring day and Bryan was waiting for her (as usual) at the entrance of the Brooklyn Botanical Garden. He was leaning against a tree, glancing through his phone. He heard her call, "Bryan!" in a distance and turned towards the sound of her voice. He saw her waving and skipping towards him, her curly weave bouncing as she did. She was wearing a yellow ruffled shirt, dark blue destroy jeans, and black high-heeled boots. She often wore heels. He didn't understand how she wore shoes so high and was still able to prance freely. He guessed she was used to the heels, after having to wear them all the time on the runway. He grinned broadly at her and waved back. He was thrilled to see her as always. His eagerness to spending time with her had not changed over the past eighteen months. They were true friends in every sense of the word and he could talk to her about almost anything. When she first told him she was a virgin and was saving herself for marriage, he was stunned. It was rare in this day and age to meet a twenty-three year old virgin, and even rarer to meet one who was a well-known model. When she shared stories about her mother's life and why she made the decision to wait, he completely understood. Before he met Rae, he never dated a girl he did not have sex with. He cared more for her to give it a shot.

Nonetheless, the past couple of months were trying for him. Initially, when they began dating, they engaged in heavy petting. It left him frustrated and brought him too close to losing his control. So, they stopped and limited their physical interaction to a light kiss on the lips and the occasional hug. Though the "no-sex" part of their relationship was challenging for both of them (particularly him), it was also very rewarding. They were able to be intimate on an entirely different level that was not physical. Since their emotions were not clouded by lust, they were genuinely able to connect intellectually and emotionally. They came to know and understand each other more than they would have if they were sleeping together.

"Hey Bryan," she said panting a little as she reached towards him to give him a quick peck on the cheek. "Sorry I'm late, the..."

"The ferry was a little late. Yeah I know." He finished the sentence for her.

"No, go away." She said jokingly and gave him a

little shove on the shoulder. "The liquor store near my place didn't have the Bordeaux wine you asked me to get. I had to get off the train in Manhattan to find it."

"Aww really? You didn't have to Rae. You could have gotten another one."

"But you really like this one and I wanted to get it for our picnic," she said pulling out the bottle from her black Michael Kors purse.

"Thanks Rae." He took the bottle from her hand and placed it in the picnic basket he placed next to his feet. He picked up the basket in one hand and grabbed her hand with the other, as he led her to a spot he chose earlier.

The spot he found was breathtaking. The grass was a vivid green color and there was a pond on one side, with cherry-blossom trees surrounding it. His timing for the picnic was perfect. It was close to dusk, and the sun cast beautiful golden rays over the area. It was after-hours and he made a private reservation; they were alone. He lay a quilt down and spread the food he brought on it; strawberries dipped in chocolate, some puff-puff, cheese and crackers, carrots and dip, and wine glasses. They sat down and chatted merrily as they sampled the food. He then pulled out a fortune cookie from the basket and handed it to her.

"This is for you, Rae-Rae. It's dessert," he said with a wink.

"Ooo," she said and stood on her knees. "I love these things, lemme see what it says." She cracked open the cookie and instead of the usual paper with some vague prophecy, there lay a glittering pear-cut diamond ring. Her eyes widened in amazement. She had not expected this at all. "Oh my goodness, Bryan. Are you for real?" She said looking up from the ring and finding him on one knee.

"I count it my luckiest good fortune to have met you. Rae, these past few months have been the happiest of my life. You make me happier than I ever thought I could be. If you let me, I want to spend the rest of my life trying to make you as happy as you make me. Raelynn Ngwa, will you do me the great honor of becoming my wife?"

Raelynn put a hand over her mouth, as tears of joy filled her eyes. After growing up in a dysfunctional home, she thought she was too damaged to experience love like this. She never thought she would be lucky enough to meet a guy like him--caring, sweet, fun, full of integrity, and attractive. She was broken in ways he did not know. Moreover, she was a criminal. She did not deserve a guy like him. She should say no. He did not deserve to marry a criminal.

On the other hand, after all she had been through, maybe she deserved a shot of happiness. Plus, her contract with Madame Josephine would be over in a few years. If she could hang on for the remaining four and a half years, she would leave in peace and Bryan would never find out.

"YES! YES! YES!" She squealed as she reached out and hugged him fiercely. He pulled back, tilted her chin up with his thumb and forefinger, and gave her a passionate kiss. When they finally pulled apart, he reached down, picked up the ring and gently slid it onto her ring finger. She held her hand with the ring up and tilted it from side to side to catch different rays of light. She squealed again and shouted, "We are engaged!" She hugged him again and whispered softly into his ear, "I love you Bryan."

"I love you too, Rae." He whispered back and kissed her on the forehead.

They spent the rest of the evening lying on the quilt, looking at the stars, and talking softly. When it got a little chilly, they cuddled under a blanket he brought and continued talking late into the night.

***

John had just reached the entrance of the company. The security guard waved at them as they drove by. He drove down a long driveway with eucalyptus trees on either side and pulled up in front of the large building. Raelynn stepped out of the car and waved to John goodbye. She walked into the two-story building and headed up the wide staircase to where Tony's office was. She knocked lightly on his door and heard a voice say, "Come in." She walked into the office and saw him sitting behind his desk, talking to someone animatedly on the phone. He raised one finger to her pleading, asking her to be patient. Raelynn nodded and walked over to one of rocking chairs in the corner and sat down. While waiting for Tony to finish, she surveyed the room, as she had done several times before. She liked the room's décor. There were paintings from various

Cameroonian artists and a bookshelf shaped into the map of Africa.

Tony hung up the phone ten minutes later in exasperation. Carlson Ache, the vice president of Marketing was one of the most irksome guys he had ever worked with. The guy did a fantastic job with advertising and selling their products in different parts of the country, but working with him on a day-to-day basis was taxing. Carlson was overly meticulous with everything and wanted to talk with Tony about every single detail. Tony was more of a big planner, kind of person. He did not like getting bogged down with details; that was more of Josh's thing. Typically, Carlson discussed all these details with Josh, but since no one knew where he was, Tony stepped up to the plate. He did not like it one bit.

He turned and looked at Rae, who was busy studying a painting on the wall. It was a simple painting of a robin sitting on a tree branch looking at a white house in the distance. He had no idea why, but she really loved that painting. He studied her for a minute. Raelynn Ngwa was unlike any other woman he ever met. Though gripped with grief and worry most of the time, she carried herself with grace and elegance he had never seen in a woman this young. She was also ingenious when it came to business. In the short time they had known one another, she made some clever suggestions about increasing their profit. And the girl knew how to dress. Though most of her clothes were dark mourning colors, she still managed to make them work with style. Today she wore a sheer black blouse with a long leather skirt with a slit to her upper thigh and dark high heels. Boy, she was hot! Even though he had seen a couple of her pictures before they met, he assumed Photoshop was exaggerating her features. Having met her in person, he realized Photoshop had nothing to do with her beauty. She was genuinely beautiful. Realizing where his thoughts were going, he quickly shook his head. He must have made some noise, because she turned around and smiled.

"Oh hi, are you done?"

"Yeah I am. Sorry about that. Carlson grates my nerves sometimes. But he's a great worker."

She chuckled softly, "Yeah it sounds like it."

"What is it about that painting that fascinates you so much?" he asked.

"What painting?"

He nodded towards the painting she had just been staring at.

"Ohhh, that one. I don't know. It seems a little whimsical, but I think the painting has a deeper meaning to it."

"Hmm, really?"

"Yeah you know. I think the bird was a pet in the house, but it eventually left home to see a different part of the world. Though it is happy to be free, it still yearned for something at its first home."

Tony nodded slowly. "Wow. I never thought of it that way. One of my sisters painted it. I doubt she was thinking about any deeper meaning like you have."

"Well, maybe not right away, but subconsciously…" A loud ring interrupted her. She pulled out her phone and saw Franck on the caller ID. "It's Franck," she explained. "I gotta take this."

"Hey massa wassup," she said into the phone.

"Rae," Franck said in a solemn voice. "Detective Asanga called."

Raelynn's heart dropped. This is it. They found Josh. Since Franck didn't sound too excited, one could only expect the worse. "Head over to the house immediately. We'll meet you there," he added before hanging up.

Raelynn slowly dropped the phone and rose to her feet. "Sorry, I gotta go."

Tony looked at her with surprise. "Wait what? Why? What did Franck say?"

"He just told me to meet him at the house."

"What's going on?"

Raelynn shrugged. "I don't know. He didn't say anything else."

"I wish I could go with you, but I have a phone meeting with those Chinese guys in thirty minutes."

"Don't worry about it Tony. It's fine. I would love to be a part of your meeting too, but…" she drifted off.

"Yeah, definitely. Meet Franck and find out what's up. I'll join you guys later at the house. But hey, let me at least walk you out."

He grabbed her elbow and led her outside to the car. He opened the door for her to get in.

"I'll see you later," he said. She simply nodded and slipped into the car. John immediately drove off at top speed.

As John pulled up to Josh's house, Raelynn spotted Franck's dark Nissan Centra and a dark Toyota Compact minivan she assumed belonged to Detective Asanga. Franck and the detective were standing in front of the main door. There were two young policemen accompanying the detective. Franck's eyes were red and brimmed with tears. She jumped out of the car, while it was still in motion and rushed up to the men on the veranda.

"What's going on? Did you find Josh?" she asked. Detective Asanga nodded and lay one hand gently on her arm.

"Miss, please let's go inside and have a seat."

Raelynn obliged and they all walked into the house. After she comfortably sat on one of the couches in the living room, she turned and looked at the detective in anticipation.

"Now can you please tell me what's going on?"

Detective Asanga took a deep breath and turned around to look at Franck, who was standing in a corner with his hand pressed tightly to his mouth; like he was trying to hold back a sob. After giving Franck a long look, he turned back to face Raelynn. She already knew what was coming. She just wanted to hear them say it.

"With the aid of a dog…" he started, "One of the guys you hired to find Josh in Buea…" he broke off again. "There's no easy way to say this, Miss. I regret to inform you that your twin brother has passed away. I'm so very sorry."

For a long moment, Raelynn sat staring into space, with tears flowing effortlessly down her cheeks.

Yet she emitted no sound. She willed herself to be strong and find out exactly what happened to Josh. Franck came over, sat next to her and wrapped an arm around her shoulders, all the while fighting back tears of his own.

"Where did you find him?" she asked in a shaky voice.

"One of the dogs your guys used to search for him found his dead body. He was buried in a shallow grave on the outskirts of Buea."

She swallowed audibly, willing herself to remain composed. "How long had he been dead?"

"The forensics team at the University of Buea Medical School are analyzing the time and cause of death, but the corpse seems to be a few weeks old. I'm so sorry for your loss Miss. We are going to do everything we can to investigate his death."

"Can I see him?" Raelynn asked after a long silence.

"Of course. One of my boys can drive you over to Buea right now. It's just after midday. You can go now and be back by 9:00 pm"

"I'm coming with you," Franck added.

Raelynn nodded and stood up. Everyone else followed. She walked outside and climbed into the police car. One of the younger policemen and Franck joined her; they drove off.

Raelynn sat in a corner of her room curled up like a ball, taking in the events of the day. She was out of tears she supposed, because she had not shed a single drop for the past few hours. This was a long time coming. Deep down, her twin intuition told her Josh was dead--that night when she had that awful dream. She barely recognized him at the forensic lab. His body was already so decomposed. She was afraid she would throw up or pass out when she saw his remains. As she looked at him, she recalled all the wonderful memories they shared. From the time they got lost in the farm when they were six, to the time their parents passed away, to their sixteenth birthday, to when she left Cameroon. Even now, she was still thinking about every single moment they shared together.

A knock interrupted her reverie. She asked for no one to disturb her for the rest of the night. She wondered who it was.

"Rae? Please open up. I know you are in there," Tony's voice said. Raelynn decided to ignore him and did not move a muscle, hoping he would get tired and go away. But he did not budge. After fifteen minutes he was still banging on the door and pleading with her to open it. She finally gave in and opened the door. His fist was raised up, ready for another knock when she swung the door open.

"Rae," he said softly and put his hand down. "How are you doing? Are you ok?"

"Am I ok?" She repeated sarcastically. "Sure. Never been better. It's not everyday one finds her twin was brutally murdered."

Tony shook his head. "My bad. I don't know what I was thinking. I'm so sorry Rae." After a little pause, he added, "May I come in?"

She shrugged and took a step back to allow him into the room.

"This is crazy! I can't believe Josh was murdered. Who would do such a thing?"

Raelynn shrugged again and sat down on her bed. There were so many emotions raging inside of her--sorrow about losing her twin, rage about how he died, and frustration about not having any clue who the murderer was.

Tony sat on the bed next to her and for a long time, there was a heavy silence between them. To his surprise, Tony heard Raelynn let out a little chuckle.

"When our mom died, Josh and I only had each other. He was so fiercely protective. I remember one time when some boys were taunting me, because I was so chubby as a kid. I remember he came to my defense and asked the boys to stop. We were only about thirteen years old and the boys were a couple of years older, like fourteen or fifteen. When they refused to stop taunting me, he got into a fight with all three of them." She chuckled again. "Such a brave and noble act, but also a little foolish. They beat him up of course, but he never stopped fighting back. Eventually, I joined him in the fight. I used my weight to smash one of the boys into the ground and Josh kicked another one so hard in the groin, he collapsed in pain. The third one ran off. Since that day, no one in the neighborhood taunted me again. Josh and I have always been a team like that." She turned and looked at him with her eyes brimming with tears. She wasn't out of tears after all, she supposed. "Why would anyone take him away from me?" She buried her face in her hands and wept. Tony put his arms around her and pulled her into his chest.

"I know Baby Girl. Some people are evil," he said soothingly, stroking one of his hands down her hair. After a while, Raelynn stopped crying, but remained in his arms. She knew it was wrong to lie in his arms like this, but it felt oddly comforting. Tony placed a soft kiss on her temple and she snuggled closer into his chest. After a moment he placed another kiss on her forehead and she tilted her head to look at him. She knew where this was headed and realized the urgency to release his embrace immediately. But somehow she could not bring herself to move. He leaned down and gave her a soft kiss on the lips. Which led to another, and then another…

***

Raelynn woke up the next morning with a pounding headache. Most of the events of the previous day felt like a dream. However, one look at the autopsy report of Josh on the side of her bed brought reality crashing down. Josh was truly gone. She vaguely remembered Tony coming to see her the night before and the evening ending with the two of them in bed together. Had that been a dream too? Or had she imagined it? One look down her body and she realized she was naked. Her scattered clothes all over the room also brought in the shattering realization that that too had not been a dream. She had never felt so mortified in all her life. How could she let this happen? Until last night, the only person she ever slept with was her husband, Bryan; and only after they got married. She was proud of that fact. Given the promiscuous culture in the United States and particularly in the entertainment industry, it was indeed a feat. All of that was now changed, because of her lapse in judgment. It is not that she felt Anthony was a bad guy, but what if down the road, they got into a relationship? What happened last night was wrong. Not only was she getting over a divorce, but also she and Tony were not planning on getting married. They were not even dating! How could he take advantage of the situation like that? She hoped he used some protection, as she was no longer on the pill. She jumped out of bed and rushed into the shower in an effort to wash away last night's memories. She wanted to forget her little tryst with Tony. She had a more important task to focus on; finding Josh's murdered. She would not rest until she avenged his death.

Raelynn saw Tony sitting on one of the couches, as soon as she walked into the living room. She groaned hoping to delay another encounter with him for as long as possible. Well, she supposed she could just get it over with. Franck was sitting next to him and they both turned their heads as they heard her walk in.

"Good morning Guys."

"Raelynn!" Tony exclaimed jumping to his feet. He cleared his throat. "How are you feeling?"

"As well as you can imagine."

Tony nodded briefly and there was an awkward silence. Franck said nothing, as he peered at both of them with suspicion in his eyes.

"Could we talk somewhere?" Tony asked. "In private?"

"Sure." She agreed.

"Excuse me Man," Tony muttered to Franck before he walked out. Raelynn followed him and they walked out to the little garden at the corner of the house.

"I want to apologize for last night; that was completely uncalled for. I came here to comfort you and wound up acting on my basic instincts. I feel like such a jerk. I'm so sorry."

"What's done is done. Let's just forget about it."

"Truth be told Rae, I have very strong feelings for you, Rae. But you are going through a lot right now and I'm sorry to add more to your plate. I just want you to know I'm always here for you and whatever you need. When you are ready, maybe we could see about us?"

She gave him a little smile. "Thanks Tony, I'd like that."

"I'm gonna head on home and try to get some sleep."

"Okay."

With that, he turned, walked back to his car, and drove off. She stayed in the garden for a moment, taking in some fresh air. When she walked back into the house, Franck was still sitting on the couch reading some document very intently. She sat down on the couch next to him and asked, "Hey you. What's that?"

"It's a copy of the police and autopsy reports about Josh. Just trying to understand all they found out."

"And?" she probed.

"Nothing much yet. They identified the murder weapon; a blunt circular object; probably a vase or something. They will return to Laura's place tomorrow to see if they can find it." He put down the paper and looked at her. "Hey, how are you doing?"

She shrugged. "I'm okay, I think. I'll be a lot better once we find who the murderer is."

He nodded in agreement. After a long pause, he added, "What's going on between you two?"

She shook her head no. "I'd rather not talk about it."

"Alright, you'll tell me when you are ready."

Eight

Raelynn drummed her fingers impatiently on Detective Asanga's desk, waiting for him to finish his call.

"Yes Sir. I'll see to that right away. He was…" he muttered into the phone. "Yes Sir."

"I wonder what his boss wants," Raelynn wondered. She considered getting another detective involved in the case, but Detective Asanga had all the details about Josh's death and he insisted he could handle the case on his own. He did not want to hand over the details of the case to some other detective, unless she talked to his boss, in which case…

"Good morning Ms. Ngwa," he said interrupting her musings. "Sorry about that. How are you doing?"

"Good morning Detective. I'm hanging in there." She cleared her throat before continuing. "I was looking through this police report and wanted to clarify something real quick."

She paused. Detective Asanga was nodding slowly and gave her a look, willing her to continue.

"You guys already searched Laura's apartment, right?"

"Laura Ade? Yeah, we sure did."

"Were there any dogs in the search party?"

"Ummm, the thing is…we had not exactly…ummmm," he stammered as he sat up straighter in his chair. "We didn't think it was necessary?"

"You mean you just wanted to save some money by doing a sloppy job with the investigation."

"Miss," he said in a reprimanding tone. "My agents and I did an excellent job in finding your brother. We…"

"It was actually one of the guys I hired who found him," she interrupted.

"The government only allocates a small budget to the police department. We can't waste all of our resources on one case."

"Then why don't you guys do a thorough job the first time, close the case, and move on?"

"We do our best."

"Which is apparently not good enough!" she fired back.

Detective Asanga sighed and lay back in his chair. "Miss Ngwa. I certainly hope you didn't come to my office today to insult me. What do you want?"

She took a deep breath. It won't do any good to irritate the man. "I would like another search done on Laura Ade's house; with dogs this time. I'll pay for the cost of the search."

He looked like he was about to argue, then resigned and gave her some paperwork to fill out. Raelynn smiled a little to herself, as she filled out all the required information. It did not matter what part of the world you lived in, money talks everywhere.

Laura stepped out of the bright yellow taxi, paid the taxi man his fare, 200FCFA and walked down the stony path to her apartment. She had a long and trying day at work and could not wait to lie down on her couch, put her feet up and drink some tea. As she approached her apartment, she heard a lot of commotion. She wondered what was going on and quickened her pace.

As soon as she turned the corner, she saw what the commotion was about. There were two police cars, as well as a private car, parked in front of her place. She recognized the private car immediately as Josh's car. Something tugged at her heart. Raelynn had to be a part of this, she mused. There were at least a dozen policemen, as well as three trained German shepherds patrolling the area. Her heart sank. She stood there for a moment, taking in the scene, like a deer stuck in headlights, until one of the policemen noticed her and pointed at her.

"OFFICER! We found her. She's right there," he yelled; that was when Laura dropped everything she was holding and ran like the wind.

Raelynn was talking with Detective Asanga and Franck when she heard the officer yelling. She immediately dropped all of her stuff too and gave chase. Almost everyone else did too. Those morning runs Raelynn did came in handy and she quickly out ran most of the policemen. Laura ran a couple of meters ahead.

Laura made a swift right turn and ran into a nearby farm. Some of the leaves in the farm were sharp and gave Raelynn many little scratches. She barely felt them and just kept running. One of the police officers in front of her stumbled on a low hanging branch and fell. She quickly jumped over him and kept running. There was now only one officer between her and Laura, and they both were rapidly closing in on her.

Laura looked back quickly to see how far they were behind her. This proved to be her undoing as she hit a rock or something and fell down. The first policeman caught up to her within seconds and used his body weight to pin her to the ground. Raelynn caught up with them a few seconds later. She pushed the police officer off Laura's back and landed a few blows on her face, all the while crying and screaming, "How dare you? How dare you? You killed my brother! You are gonna pay for this! You shrew!!"

"Get off of me!" Laura yelled, as she raised her hands to her face to deflect Raelynn's punches. All the while, the police officer tried in vain to separate them. He thought about lifting Raelynn off Laura's back, but feared Laura would use the opportunity to escape. A minute later, the second officer caught up with them. One of them pulled Raelynn off Laura. The other handcuffed Laura and told her she was under arrest. He roughly pulled her up to her feet and urged her forward.

"Under arrest for what?" she asked calmly.

"For the murder of Josh Ngwa on the 27th of September."

"I didn't kill anyone. There has to be some kind of mistake."

"A mistake?" Raelynn screeched in a glass shattering tone. "Are you still denying it? You got to be kidding me."

"I loved Josh with all my heart. I didn't kill him."

"Please stop with the lies. We found the murder weapon buried in your backyard, as well as both of your clothes covered in his blood."

Laura's eyes widened. Before she could say anything, Detective Asanga and two other officers joined them.

"Serge, Eric, and Sebastien, accompany this woman to the station," Detective Asanga ordered. "I called the lieutenant, he's waiting for you. Now go."

The three officers he called quickly pushed Laura forward and dragged her to the police car. All the while Laura cried out, "I didn't do it! I didn't kill Josh! You have to believe me."

Raelynn watched as they dragged Laura off. She leaned against a plantain tree and let out a sigh of relief. Now justice was served. She avenged her twin. Though there was nothing she could do to bring him back from the dead, the least she could do was make sure his murderer was put away. She would personally make sure Laura spent the rest of her life locked up.

Detective Asanga gave her a gentle squeeze on the shoulder. "It's alright Ms. Ngwa. We got her. Everything is going to be fine."

"No, everything is definitely not fine," Raelynn thought. Josh was still dead and her heart was broken into a million pieces. She did not say anything to the detective. She slightly nodded to him, as he walked past her to rejoin the rest of his team.

Raelynn thought she experienced pain and sorrow at her mom's burial a decade ago. It did not compare to how she felt now at Josh's funeral service. The wake the previous night was just as painful. Hundreds of people flocked by to mourn and discuss the life of the young man, Josh. All kinds of rumors were flying about his death. Some suggested Laura used witchcraft to kill him. Others said his enemies sent evil spirits into Laura that possessed her to commit murder. Still others rumored Josh cheated on Laura with another girl, which caused Laura to kill him out of rage. Raelynn did not try to correct any of the rumors she heard. It did not matter what they said. It did not matter what Laura's motives were. Josh was dead and nothing was going to change that.

At the funeral service, she listened as Tita read Josh's eulogy. She glanced down the pew at Ma Bridget and saw her wiping her tears away. It seemed like Ma Bridget had not stopped crying since Raelynn went to Santa (a small village) to tell her the news of Josh's death. She looked so old, fragile, and miserable Raelynn thought she would shatter. Ma Bridget caught her staring and gave her a weak smile and turned her head towards the altar to pay attention to what Tita was saying. When the time came for Raelynn to give a few remarks, she choked up so many times that it took a while for her to get through her speech, which was warm and heartfelt. After Raelynn finished, the congregation cried buckets of tears.

When service ended, a couple of Josh's friends carried the coffin with his remains out to the cemetery. The pastor, elders, and close family and friends walked closely behind them. Raelynn, Tita, Lum, Anthony, Franck, and a handful of other people had sewn different outfits with the same material. The material had a combination of green, gold, and white with a recent picture of Josh in the front along with the dates of his birth and death below it. Above the picture was written: IN LOVING MEMORY OF JOSH NTI NGWA. When they got to the cemetery, a few young men dug up a hole and lowered the coffin into it. The pastor said a few more words before he asked Ma Bridget to throw in a handful of dirt, as was their custom. With the aid of her cane, Ma Bridget walked slowly to the edge and picked up a handful of soil. Before she tossed it in, she fell on her knees and wailed loudly. Raelynn came to her side. She also fell on her knees, threw an arm around her great grand aunt's shoulders, and wept with her. Raelynn then urged Ma Bridget to let go of the soil she was holding. When Ma Bridget finally did, Raelynn picked up a handful too and slowly threw it on top of the coffin. "Good-bye my Darling brother. I'll miss you. I really hope you are in better place." A few other close friends and family each threw in a handful of dirt. Then the diggers filled up the hole and it was over. There was a huge reception after the burial with lots of food and traditional dances. However, Raelynn's mind went blank, and the rest of the day was a haze.

Raelynn tossed and turned in her bed. She did not feel so good. She had been under the weather for the past week. She needed to see a doctor if this persisted. She bolted from her bed and ran to the bathroom, as a wave of nausea overcame her. She retched the little food she had managed to eat during breakfast. She lost almost five pounds this week. Initially, she thought she had food poisoning or something. Then she assumed she was just tired. No amount of sleep or rest made her feel better. When it did not pass after a few days, she thought she had a cold, but she had no other cold symptoms: no fever, no nasal discharge, no headaches, etc. She felt weak all the time and threw up everything she ate. Out of curiosity, she pulled out her phone and Googled, 'Why am I always throwing up?' She clicked on the first link that appeared. The first suggestion read 'morning sickness'. Her heart raced. This idea completely escaped her mind. No, she could not be pregnant, right? Since she came to Cameroon two months ago, she had not been sexually active, except that one fateful night with Tony. She thought he used protection. She could not be pregnant, right? Those things were supposed to be very efficient, right? She realized with another sinking feeling it had been more than a month since she had her period. She had to make sure. She dialed one of her childhood friends, Rita that she recently reconnected with.

"Hey Gurl," she answered cheerily on the fifth ring. "How are you feeling?"

"Ehhhh about the same. Could you please do me a favor?"

"Yeah sure, Hun. Whatever you need."

"Could you please come by my house as soon as you can?" After a pause, she added. "Bring a pregnancy kit with you?"

"Gurl what??? You get belle? When did this happen? How many months now? You just got here. Who's the father?"

"Ri, please calm down. I'm not sure yet. Just checking. Could you just bring over the kit please?"

"Yeah sure, I'll be there in half an hour."

"Thanks Dear," Raelynn said and then she hung up the phone.

"How long has it been?" Raelynn asked impatiently, as she paced up and down her bedroom. Rita looked at her watch again. "It's only been over a minute. We'll know the results in another minute."

Raelynn put her fingertips on her temple and gently massaged them. "She could not imagine being pregnant. Even when she was happily married to Bryan, she did not plan on having children for at least three years. She did not want to be the cliché single mother that was becoming a trend these days. She wanted her kid to feel secure, loved, and grow up with both parents. She had been so careful before, if only…"

"It's time." Rita said, interrupting her thoughts. Raelynn quickly walked up to the pregnancy stick and picked it up. It was "Positive."

Anthony Mbah sat in one of the most popular chicken parlors in Yaoundé, nursing a bottle of Guinness Smooth. As far as chicken parlors go in Cameroon, it was splendid. The peach couch he was sitting on was fairly new and comfortable. There were two paintings of flowers on two of the walls in the room and a small coffee table with a radio on top of it in the center. The radio was playing classic makossa and Anthony nodded along, swaying gently to the beat of the music. Raelynn was half an hour late. This did not surprise him because she was always late for one reason or another. He wondered what she had to say to him so privately. Ever since their one night together she avoided him. When they did meet, she was elusive and always found an excuse to leave.

Josh left her with more than half of his property; not that she needed it anyway She had enough money of her own. Josh willed Laura another 25% and the remaining percentage to Ma Bridget.

Raelynn had not stopped by the firm to see how business was doing since Josh was found dead. Not that he really cared, he was managing the business fine on his own. He had to admit he missed her. Their previous conversations were exhilarating and he found her irresistibly attractive. He was hoping all this detachment was her way of properly mourning Josh and that soon she would return to her normal self. He missed Josh too, but losing one's business partner and losing a twin were two different things.

He was pleasantly surprised when she texted him the other night and asked him to meet her. He heard a knock on the door before it opened. A middle-aged woman with a dull black dress and white apron walked in. Raelynn was directly behind her.

"*Le voici Mademoiselle. Amusez vous,*" the waitress said, as she gave a little bow and left the room, shutting the door behind her.

"*Merci beaucoup, Madame,*" replied Raelynn before she turned towards Tony and said, "Heyy."

He stood up from the couch and gave her a long hug. Initially, she stood stiffly and did not return the hug, but eventually she relaxed and hugged him back.

"She looks a little tired," he thought. She also looked like she lost a few pounds. She could not afford to lose any weight. She was already so slender. If she lost any more weight, she would look malnourished.

"How are ya? It's been a while. Please have a seat," Tony said, after breaking up the hug.

"I know right? It has been a while. I have been a little preoccupied," Raelynn said taking a seat on the couch across from him.

"I can only imagine. Are you doing alright?" He asked with concern in his voice. "You look a bit tired."

"Just been a little under the weather lately. I'll be fine. Thanks for your concern."

Just then another waiter came in and took Raelynn's order. She ordered roasted macquerel fish with dodo and a bottle of Orangina to drink. Tony tried engaging her in conversation a few times, but it was obvious something was on her mind. She kept asking him to repeat everything he said. After the waiter served their meals, Tony asked, "Ok c'mon Raelynn, what's going? Is something bothering you?"

"Ummm yeah…there is something I want to tell you." She leaned back in the chair, crossed her legs and covered her face with one hand. Then without preamble, she exclaimed, "I'm pregnant!"

For a long moment, there was silence. They could hear the voices of other people laughing in the next room. Tony was shocked. Of all the things he could have expected her to say, this was the least he anticipated. They had only been together that one night.

"Is it mine?" he asked hesitantly. He had to make sure.

"Yeah." She answered with exasperation. How could he even ask that? "I haven't been with anyone else since I came home."

"But---ttt—tt how? I used protection."

Raelynn hugged herself, "I don't know. But you know those things aren't 100% effective. These things happen."

Tony stood to his feet. "I can't believe this." He started pacing around the tiny space. Then he walked over to her, sat down, and took one of her hands in both of his. "But heyyy…It'll be alright. I'm sorry it's my fault you are going through this. I want you to know that whatever you want to do with this pregnancy, you have my full support. I'm here for you."

Raelynn gave his hand a gentle squeeze. "Thanks Anthony, I really appreciate it."

Although the news was shocking, Anthony was thrilled she was pregnant. He knew he wanted to be with Raelynn Ngwa for a long time. He actually fantasized about them being a couple. He hoped she kept the pregnancy.

"Do you know what you want to do with the pregnancy?"

She took a deep breath and slowly nodded. "Yeah." Pause. "I think I'm gonna keep it."

"That's great! Wow, I'm going to be a father. I can't believe it."

"I want you to know you don't have any obligations to me or this child. I just thought you should know about the baby."

"Thanks for letting me know. Of course, I want to be part of our baby's life, and a part of his or her mother's life too," he said with a wry smile. "If you'll give me a chance," he added. Raelynn smiled back at him and replied. "Yeah, I'd like that."

Even though she had not planned to get pregnant, she was falling in love with the little human growing inside of her. She never dreamed she could love someone she never met before as much. It was amazing.

Nine

Raelynn plopped a piece of pineapple into her mouth and closed her eyes in ecstasy. Mmmm it was so good. All the fruits in the United States had nothing on the tropical fruits here in Cameroon. She particularly enjoyed paw-paws, pineapples, and mangoes. She put another piece of fruit into her mouth before she leaned back into the comfortable office chair and rubbed her baby bump. She was four months along now and thank goodness the morning sickness phase passed.

She was sitting in Tony's office waiting for him to come back from an emergency. One of the major water pumps in the firm had malfunctioned and leaked water everywhere. The excess water could damage the packaged cement ready for sale. Many at the firm tried to save the cement, while the rest tried to fix the pump. Someone called a technician to help, while everyone else struggled to minimize the damage. She offered to help, but Tony would not hear of it. Lifting bags of cement was not a woman's work, and besides she was pregnant. He did not want to risk her having a miscarriage or harming the pregnancy in any way. Thus, she sat in Tony's office for over an hour entertaining oneself.

She was extremely bored now and stood up. She walked slowly around the room, looking at the pictures and books she had seen a thousand times. None of the books he had interested her. She walked back to his chair behind the office desk and sank into it. She opened the drawers idly and browsed at the contents. One drawer had a stack of papers in it and other materials; another had a bunch of snacks: chin-chin, coconut sweet, chips, nuts, and the like. She helped herself to some chin-chin and peanuts. She tried to open one of the smaller top drawers, but it was locked. "This is a little weird, because all the other drawers were not." She dismissed the thought. He probably had some important documents or something in there that he did not want laying around.

She picked up one of the books on his shelf, *Reengineering the Corporation* and tried to read it. After fifteen minutes of staring at the same page, she gave up and put the book back in it's place. She drew her attention back to the locked drawer. Just out of curiosity she wanted to see what was in it.

One voice in her head said, "You should leave the drawer alone", while another probed her to "check it out." She gave in to the latter voice. After all her years of stealing and conning people, she learned a trick or two about opening up locked doors, drawers, cars, etc. She took a paper clip from the top of his desk and expertly maneuvered it to open the drawer. She pulled it out and found an iPad in it. There was nothing else in the drawer. She picked up the iPad, all the while thinking she should not be snooping into his things. For a split second, she almost put it back. But boredom and curiosity got the best of her and she turned the iPad on. She found dozens of documents of client accounts. This was not a crime she thought, after all, she owned almost half of the company now. Thus far, Tony made most of the business decisions by himself. It would not hurt to go over some of the accounts to keep her self abreast. She opened one of the folders labeled Owen Michael. A quick glance showed nothing out of order. It was when she started reading the details that she saw it. Her eyes popped in shock. What the…

Just then she heard Tony talking in the hallway, his footsteps getting closer and stronger. She quickly turned off the iPad, put it back in its place and closed the drawer. By the time Tony got into the room, she was sitting comfortably in his chair with her feet on the desk looking at something intently on her phone. One would never guess what she had been up to seconds ago. But of course she was a pro; snooping had been part of her job description.

"Hey Rae. I'm so sorry for the wait." He apologized, as he leaned down towards her and gave her a kiss on the cheek.

"It's ok. I understand. These things happen. Is everything ok now?"

He nodded and put a hand behind his neck and gently massaged the muscles there. "Yeah, everything is fine now. Thank goodness the technician fixed the leak." He leaned on his desk next to her. "What have you been up to?"

"Nothing much," she lied. "Just browsing on my phone."

"Alright. Do you still wanna grab something to eat? Or we could just go home."

She shrugged. "Whatever you want. I already snacked on some of the goodies you got here and I also ate some fruit. I'm not really hungry." "I'm a deadbeat. Let's go to my place then and just chill." He helped her to her feet and they grabbed their belongings. He had his hand on the small of her back as they walked out. "Maybe I can even get you to spend the night this time," he added winking at her.

"Not a chance." She retorted.

"See, I don't get that. We are dating now. We even have a child on the way. Why are you still holding out?"

Of course he would not understand. Most guys did not. She was very old-fashioned when it came to things like that. She believed a couple should only get sexually intimate after they were married or at the very least engaged. She saw so many women suffer the consequences of premarital sex for her to take it lightly; the unwanted pregnancies, children out of wedlock, abortions, some of which resulted in infertility, panging after a man for years after he moved on to the next hot thing, the STDs, etc. Just look at what had happened with her mother. She was determined not to follow in her mother's footsteps. Ironically, the same thing that happened to her mother happened to her; getting pregnant out of wedlock. Though she made that mistake once and now had to face dire consequences, she was not willing to make the same mistake again. She would not go down that road.

Bryan was one of the few guys she knew who understood her position, which had made her love him all the more. He was willing to wait until he put a ring on her finger before they made love. Tony was not as understanding. For one thing he knew she was not a virgin. But he also did not know she had been married and had lost her virginity to her ex-husband.

After seeing what was hidden in that folder, there was a lot she had to find out about him before even considering to take things to the next level. She said simply, "I'm not ready yet."

"Do you have any idea when you'll be ready?"

She shook her head. "No. I'll let you know when I am." She stopped walking and waited until he turned around and quirked an eyebrow at her. "Look Tony, I thought I made this clear before. I don't want you to be in a relationship with me because of our baby. If you don't think you can wait, we might as well call the relationship off."

"Of course not, Sweetheart. I'm sorry. I didn't mean to pressure you."

Tony remained baffled. He had been with a number of girls before and none of them held out on sex for so long. Maybe they did for the first or second date, but by the third date, it was on. Now he had been on at least a dozen dates with Raelynn and the girl was not shaking. She was not a virgin either, so it did not make any sense to him. Or had she been assaulted? The one night they shared was passionate. She did not seem like someone who was scared of sexual intimacy. What was her deal now? It did not matter anyway. If she wanted him to wait, he would wait. Sooner or later she would be his.

Raelynn peeked into the office and found Franck looking intently at a large piece of paper; it was probably some architectural design. Franck got his degree in architecture at the University of Buea a few years ago and was currently working in a small architectural firm in Yaoundé. He had his back to her and was so caught up with the design that he did not hear her slowly open the door and walk in. She stood there for a few minutes, waiting to see if he would notice her

"Mmm hmm." She finally said. He jumped and quickly turned around.

"Raelynn!!!" he exclaimed and walked over to give her a hug. "What are you doing here?"

"Just in the neighborhood. I brought lunch, I thought you might be interested."

"For real?? Aww, you are too sweet. Let's go to the conference room," he said as he urged her out of the office and closed the door.

"What were you working on?" she asked as they made their way to the conference room.

"Ohh, you know, just normal stuff. That was a design of a really old building and my boss wanted me to take a look at it, so the city counsel can determine if the building should be remolded or if they should tear it down. I was checking out the electrical components and all that stuff. Don't wanna bore you with all the details. Let's talk about you, Rae. How are you? It's been a while."

They continued to chat blissfully, as they got to the conference room and Raelynn laid out the little feast she had brought. There was some ndole, dodo (sliced fried plantains), suya, white yams, some fruits as well as a few bottles of Malta to drink.

"Oh my goodness. Seriously?" He cried after she placed everything on the table. "Are you having a party? Or are you just trying to get me fat?"

Raelynn shrugged. "You can have a little of everything. I want you to have a choice."

He shook his head and laughed, as he helped himself to some ndole and white yams.

"How is the pregnancy by the way? Everything good?"

"Oh yeah. I met my doctor yesterday and everything looks fine. Thank goodness, I'm done with the first trimester. No more morning sickness."

"That's great Rae. Do you know if it's gonna be a boy or girl?"

"Not yet," she replied taking a sip of water. "We'll know in a few weeks."

Out of the blue she asked, "What do you think of Tony?"

Franck gave her a look of surprise. "How do you mean?"

"I mean what do you think of him personally."

Franck placed his fork down and wiped his mouth with a napkin. "Where is this coming from?" he asked seriously.

"I just want to know what you think of him. And please don't sugarcoat how you feel about him, because we are having a baby together or because we are dating. I want your honest opinion."

He cleared his throat. "Well, if you really want to know." He took a deep breath. I don't trust him. Never have."

"Why?"

"I don't know. I can't really explain it. There's just something a little off about him. Don't get me wrong he seems charming and sensitive all the time. I have a feeling he's been devious about something. I just can't place my finger on it. But, hey that's just what I think personally. Why do you ask?"

She lowered her voice and proceeded to tell him what she had found in his office.

"Well dang," he exclaimed. "That's just criminal. What are you going to do? You own half of the company. Do you think Josh was part of it?"

She shrugged. "I don't know. But I intend to find out."

He leaned back in his chair and sighed. "This is so crazy. I've always had the feeling he's not up to anything good."

Raelynn shrugged, "Yep, that's the father of my child."

"How did that happen anyway? When did you guys start shacking up? You never told me. I know you don't normally do hookups."

"I'd rather not talk about it. And yeah I don't do hookups. That was a mistake. It won't happen again."

"Even now that you guys are dating?"

"Yep."

"Kudos to you Girl. Mistakes happen, with consequences sometimes. But it's great to see that you are keeping your standards." After a brief pause, he added. "Are you going to continue seeing him?"

She shrugged again, "I don't know. At least for the time being until I figure out what he is up to with our clients. It'll be easier to find out stuff from him if we are dating."

He nodded in agreement, and then remembered something. "Ooo, what happened to the Naija guy, Bryan you were seeing? Sounded like you really liked him."

Of course, Raelynn had not told anyone in Cameroon, except Josh that she had gotten married. She made him swear to keep it a secret without really explaining why. With the Internet and social media, news spread very quickly. She did not want Madame Josephine to even hear a rumor that she was married. Madame Josephine would investigate who her husband was. If she ever found out the truth, Raelynn would be toast. When people asked her about her relationship status, she simply said she was involved with a Naija guy, Bryan, without saying his last name or showing a picture.

"That didn't work out," she replied.

"Oh man, I'm so sorry Rae," Franck said sympathetically. "It was probably for the best."

"Yeah, it was," she said sadly.

Raelynn chose the time perfectly. She invited Tony to her place so she could make him dinner. It was a Friday night, so he did not have to rush home to get ready for work the next morning. While she made dinner, she gave him several bottles of his favorite beer, Export Lite. He went to the bathroom a couple of times.

Every time he did, he took his phone with him. It was so frustrating. She had to get him to leave her with his phone for a few minutes. So she tried another tactic.

"Ohhh no…my phone is about to die. Do you mind if I borrow your phone, Darling? I need to make a call."

"Ummmm, yeah sure." He replied and took the phone out of his back pocket and handed it to her. "Here you go."

"Thanks Dear," she said sweetly and dialed Franck's number.

"Helloo…Franck? How far?"

"Rae?" A voice said into the phone. *"I dey ooo. Weti di happen?"*

"Nothing much. *I bi just want ask you about that my thing,"* she said walking into the pantry like she was going to get something.

"What thing?"

"You know. We talked about this yesterday. I need it tomorrow," she continued as she connected the phone to *Twista*, the device she used when she worked for Madame Josephine to copy information from peoples' phones. She hid it behind the cereal boxes earlier. Thanks goodness she thought to bring this cunning device home with her. All it needed was a minute to fully copy the information. She hoped Tony would not get suspicious.

"What thing?" Franck asked again, having no clue what she was talking about.

"C'mon Bruhh. You promised nahh."

"Oh right yeah, of course. My bad, I'll bring it tomorrow." Franck still had no clue what she talking about. But he decided to play along. "Do you need anything else?"

"Nahh that's all. Could you bring it over by 10:00 am in the morning?" she replied while looking at the completion bar on the device. It was half way full.

"For sure. I got you."

"Thanks Franck. How much do I owe you for this?"

"Two million dollars," he said outrageously.

Raelynn was nervous that Tony would walk in on her at any moment, but she managed to chuckle a little at what Franck had said.

"That's a little steep, but you got it. I only have half the cash on me. Can I write you a check?"

"Yeah, sure that is fine. What about lunch next Thursday?"

"That sounds great," Raelynn said absentmindedly. She checked the status of the bar and it was now 98%. She watched it became 100%. Then after a few seconds, she quickly disconnected the device and hid it back behind the cereal boxes. "Where you do you want to go?" she added, as she grabbed some palm oil and crayfish and walked out of the pantry. She deliberately left those items in the pantry, so she would have an excuse to go get them later. She found Tony sitting on the same counter stool she left him on. He helped himself to some fresh corn and groundnuts she put out for a snack.

"We can hash out the details later. Are you good?"

"Never better. I'll talk to you later. Thank you so much."

"Anytime Rae. My pleasure. See ya later, bye."

"Bye Franck," she said hanging up and handing the phone back to Tony. "Thank you. We just had to sort that out."

"No problem Rae. Found what you were looking for in there?"

"Yeah, I just wanted to add some palm oil flavor to the cornchaff (a Cameroonian delicacy). You know cornchaff isn't complete until you add crayfish."

He simply smiled. *"That one dey.* What's up with Franck?"

"He helped me buy one of my favorite perfumes from Douala. I couldn't find it anywhere out here. He's bringing it tomorrow." She reached out and smoothed both her hands down his shoulders.

"Oh okay." To her relief, he did not ask any more questions about her conversation with Franck.

She plugged *Twista* into her laptop and waited for it to load. Everything from Anthony's phone came up. The hackers working with Madame Josephine could crack up everything from this information, including hidden bank passwords and the like. They could even access his email.

Unfortunately, she was not a hacker so she could not do all the fancy stuff. She could see all his messages, including the ones he deleted. The hackers probably had a code to categorize the messages, but she did not know how to do that either. She sighed and started pouring through thousands of messages, which were in no particular order. After two hours, she began to feel hopeless. Maybe there was nothing in here about Josh's involvement with Mr. Owen. She closed her laptop, climbed into bed and went to sleep.

A few hours later, she suddenly woke up and could not go back to sleep. It was three o'clock in the morning. She went down to the kitchen and got herself a glass of strawberry-banana smoothie and walked back to her room. She sat on her bed and stared at her laptop for a couple of minutes, while drumming her fingers on her thighs. She reached out and grabbed it and continued pouring through the text messages. After thirty minutes or so, she found something under the deleted messages.

'Hey Man, I wanted to tell you this earlier. I don't think I can do this anymore.'

'Do what anymore?'

'Lie to our clients. It's just wrong. We gotta stop.'

'Are you kidding me? Do you know how much money we will lose? Where is all this coming from?'

'Ever since I became a Christian, my conscience has been weighing heavily on me. We have to come clean.'

'Conscience my foot. Gimme a break. It's that girl Laura who has been putting things into your head.'

'Nahh, she has nothing to do with this. She has no idea about what's going on with my clients. It's entirely my decision.'

'We need to talk about this. Are you already in Buea?'

'Yeah, I'm at her place.'

'Alright, I stopped in Edea to stretch my legs. I'll turn the car around and head back to Buea. We need to talk about this in person.'

'Yeah, we do. I'll see you in a few hours then.'

The messages were post dated October 15, which was the day before Josh disappeared. It was also the day before his blood was found all over Laura's living room. Anthony lied. He failed to mention he drove back to Buea to meet with Josh after he dropped him off in Douala a few hours earlier. Why did he lie about something like this? Unless he had something to hide…

Ten

Raelynn walked into the police district in Buea and saw two middle-aged men at the counter. She had been there so many times before that most of the policemen in the district knew her by name.

"Good morning, Miss Ngwa," one of them called out as she entered. "What brings you by?"

"Good morning Officers," she replied cheerily. "I was wondering if you had the items Josh Ngwa was wearing when he was found?"

The officers quietly whispered to one another; then one of them checked the computer records.

"Yeah Miss. We got them. Even though a suspect for Josh Ngwa's murder has been tried and sentenced, we keep all evidence for five years after the case is solved just in case there is some dispute or if there is a need for a future trial. Why do you ask?"

"There was an Apple watch among his things. I would like to borrow it for a few hours. I'll bring it right back."

"I'm afraid we can't do that Miss. Only a forensic scientist, pathologist, or lawyer involved in the case has access to those items. Anyone else must bring a signed order from a judge."

"Of course, I understand. Is there no other way? It's just a watch. What evidence can it possibly give?"

"I'm sorry Miss. There's nothing we can do."

"Will this help you change your minds?" She slid 500,000 FCFA across the counter to them. "I'll have the watch for a couple of hours, then I'll bring it right back."

The officers looked at each other again and one of them quickly slipped the money into his back pocket and nodded. "In that case, we can work something out. Here, fill out and sign this form." One of them handed her a sheet of paper, and while she filled it out, the other one went to the storage to get the watch in question. A few moments later, he returned with the watch in a blue evidence bag.

"Could you sign here please?" the other officer urged. She looked down at where he was pointing and signed the document quickly.

"Alright, here you go Ms. Ngwa," he said and took the bag from the other officer and handed it to her. "You have twenty-four hours. Come back here with the watch tomorrow at this same time."

"You got it. Thanks Officers," Raelynn said, as she picked up the evidence bag. "I'll bring it back here same time tomorrow."

Raelynn knew she was searching for a needle in the haystack, as she held the watch in her gloved hands with Josh's blood on it. She felt nauseous, but forced herself to be strong. Surprisingly, the watch worked splendidly after she charged it. "Apple products can stand the test of time, huh?" she thought.

She remembered sending him this watch on their last birthday, July 10. It was Apple's latest watch design, built with a microphone and speaker that could record a six-hour conversation with a single click. She bought it for him, because he once mentioned he needed a recording device that was easy to record all his clients' wishes in explicit detail, then he could later listen more closely, if necessary. He also wanted to hear how he sounded, while talking with his clients and employers to improve his bargaining techniques. So she surprised him with this new Apple watch, which at the time, had not officially launched. She was able to get it, because one of Apple's CEOs regularly visited the Moreau companies. Raelynn cozied up to him one day and got a copy when he returned on his next visit to Moreau's office building. Josh absolutely loved it. The smile on his face was priceless, when he Face Timed her to say thank you. She hoped the watch recorded something during the hours leading up to his death to give her a clue of what really happened.

She turned the watch in her hands and scrolled left on the home page to access the recorded messages. She clicked the tab key. After briefly scanning her face on the phone's screen, it read, ERROR please try again. Raelynn sighed, because she realized Josh used a face recognition software to access all his personal data. Thank goodness she had Twista. It should work on an Apple watch. She connected the watch to Twista and waited for it to copy all the information. Afterwards, she transferred the information to her laptop.

Fortunately for her, the recorded messages were not encrypted so she could listen to any of them. But as usual, the messages were not in any particular order. She had to comb through a bunch of them before she found a recording for that day, September 27th. She walked to her bedroom door to make sure it was closed before she sat down again on her chair. She took a deep breath and pressed play.

She heard two voices. There was so much static she could not identify the voices clearly, much less what they said. After a couple of seconds, the voices became clearer and she heard:

'What the heck Man? You just hit me on the head. I'm bleeding. Get me to the hospital.' The voice coughed and groaned in pain. (It was Josh's voice. There was no doubt about it). She heard a cynical laughter and then sounds of someone banging an object against what she only imagined was probably Josh's head. She flinched with each blow. Finally, the groaning stopped and she heard another voice. 'We'll see about that. Dead men tell no tales.' (This time it was Tony's voice). After that she heard sounds of someone grunting and dragging something heavy and then a loud thud, which sounded like the trunk of a car being slammed shut. After that there was silence.

Raelynn got up, ran to her bathroom and threw up. Josh was smart enough to tape his murder to show who was responsible. They arrested the wrong person. Anthony murdered her brother.

Two days later, Raelynn was in the upstairs study going over all of Tony's messages from his phone and the recordings from Josh's watch. Since the day she found out the truth about Anthony, she had been violently sick. She was not able to get out of bed for a whole day; she felt dizzy and she could not eat anything. Lum took her to the hospital earlier that day. The only reason she agreed to go was because she did not want anything bad to happen to her baby. His father might be a psycho and a murderer, but the baby was still a part of her and had nothing to do with his father. Anthony tried calling her, but she would not pick up any of his calls. He stopped by yesterday to check on her, but she asked Lum to tell him she was asleep and could not be disturbed. She did not have the courage or heart to face him yet.

She felt a lot better now because of the medication the doctor prescribed. She now sat in her office in the house, trying to gather as much evidence as she could to take to the police station: messages from phone and voice recordings from the watch. Lum went out with some friends, and she gave the housekeeper and the driver a night off. So she was home alone. She was so caught up with what she was doing that she did not notice when Tony entered the house, until he opened the door of the study. When she looked up and saw him, she shrieked. "Oh my goodness, Tony? You scared me half to death. What are you doing here?"

"Can't a fellow surprise his girlfriend?" He said as he strode further into the room.

"Well, yeah I guess. You really did surprise me."

"Are you feeling a lot better, Hun?" He asked.

"Yeah I guess I am. I'll be alright."

She replied, trying to sound as normal as possible and not betray the fact that she wanted to shoot him in the head. He came by and sat down in the chair across from the desk. She tried to say something, but could not bring herself to say anything. Nor did he. For a long moment, they just stared at each other from across the desk. His gaze was steady and even.

"So you know, huh?" he finally said. She shook her head. He could not possibly be talking about Josh. Was she that easy to read?

"Know what?"

"Don't play dumb with me Baby Girl. I know that you know."

"Know what?" she asked, as she continued to feign ignorance.

"About what happened to Josh."

Her heartbeat increased. Another look into his eyes chilled her. How could he possible know she found out his secret so soon? This was not good. She tried to remember where she kept her phone, so she could dial Franck or the police. Then she remembered she had left her phone on the charger in her bedroom.

"Why?" she asked. He sighed and walked over to the side of her desk, leaned a hip against the edge, and crossed one ankle over the other. "Josh and I had a good thing going. It was perfect."

"You mean stealing hundreds of thousands of francs from your clients?" she interjected. He laughed.

"Yeah, I guess you can put it like that. And then all of a sudden, he becomes a Christian and doesn't want to play anymore." He let out a sigh of disgust.

"So you killed him for that?"

"Well…not just for that. I'm not that heartless you know. He not only wanted to stop conning our clients, he wanted us to give back all the money we had taken from them. Not only would that bankrupt us, but we would also go to jail. I wasn't willing to take that chance. This pretty face ain't ready for no jail. I drove over to Laura's to try to reason with him and talk some sense into his head. But he wouldn't listen. So I killed him." Tony said it so casually as though he was talking about the weather.

"And you framed Laura."

"Oh yeah. Someone had to be responsible for his death you know. Being at Laura's place when it all happened made things so convenient. All I had to do was take one of her blouses from of her closet, rub it with his blood, and bury it in her backyard with the vase I used to hit him. You guys fell so hard for it," he laughed. "Everything would have been fine if you would've let *sleeping dogs lie*. But no, you had to *shake the boat*."

"You truly are evil."

He shrugged. "Maybe I am. Whatever. I watch out for my own interests."

"How did you figure out what I was up to?" She had to know.

"Ohhh, Sweetheart, you really tried not to betray your thoughts. If it were anyone else, they wouldn't have figured it out. But you can't fool me. I started suspecting something the day I left you in my office alone for a long while. It wasn't until you invited me to dinner last week that I knew something was up. You were being flirtatious, which isn't something you normally do. I've been in your pantry before. It doesn't take as long as it took you to find crayfish and palm oil. They would've been right in the front. So I planted a few cameras around the house to watch you. Two days ago, a little birdie told me you knew the truth about Josh. I'm still not sure how you did it, but all that matters is I know that you know. I have one question for you. How did you figure it out? What does that device do?"

She shook her head slowly. "I'm not telling you that."

Something akin to anger flashed in his eyes for a second, and then it was gone. "Ehhh, it doesn't matter anyways."

"What are you going to do to me?" she asked hesitantly.

"You already know. I can't have any loose ends."

"Doesn't the fact that I'm carrying your child mean anything to you?"

"Yeah believe me it kinda does. It was a pleasant surprise you got pregnant. It would have been perfect if you had already given birth. By getting rid of you afterwards, the child would inherit all you own, which implies I would own the whole company."

She swallowed audibly. "You were planning to get rid of me whether I found out the truth or not?"

"No, if you had not poked your nose into other people's business, all would be fine. I would have convinced you to marry me and gotten full control of the firm any way."

She shook her head slowly. "Did you ever even like me?"

"I can't really say. I fancied you and I enjoyed your company. I thought you were really hot, I still do. Having you as a life partner would have been really nice."

"Anthony, you don't have to do this. I have enough money to buy the whole company. I can give it to you. You can use the money to escape and start a new life in a new place. Somewhere far, far, away."

He scoffed. "You expect me to believe that? If I let you leave this room, you are gonna have me arrested."

"I'm not. I swear. You have my word."

"Unfortunately Babe, your word means absolutely nothing to me." He stood up quickly, reached down, and wrapped both of his hands around her neck and squeezed. Raelynn started gasping for air and remembered one of the defense moves Josh taught her. She reached up and kicked him squarely in the groin. His hands left her neck, as he bent over in pain. She seized the opportunity to get off the chair, ran out of the study, and headed for her bedroom.

As she reached behind to close the door, she felt Anthony push it from the other side. She screamed at the top of her lungs, in hopes that her neighbors heard her screams and would come to her rescue. Anthony continued pushing against the door, while with all her strength she tried to overcome him. But he was much bigger and stronger than she was. After a while, he swung the door open and walked into her room. His hands went around her neck again. This time the pressure was stronger. She struggled in an attempt to kick, scratch, or punch him. He pushed her until her head hit a wall and he lifted her off her feet, all the while increasing the pressure in his hands. Raelynn saw everything go black, as she slipped into oblivion and passed out.

As Anthony walked out of the house, he saw an elderly couple standing by the entrance looking at the house with concern.

"Wuna dey fine for that house?" the woman asked. "We heard a scream."

"Oh no. Everything is fine. My girlfriend is a little dramatic. We were playing a run and catch game, and she got a little excited."

"Hmmm," the elderly woman said smiling. *"Young love ooo."* She turned and looked at her husband. "Marcus, how come we don't do that anymore?"

"Ma Bea, abeg ooo. You don ova old. If I start follow you, you go fall break your head oo. I no wan kill my wife."

The woman pretended to be offended and smacked him lightly on the arm. *"Ok, wunna goodnight ooo."* the woman said to Tony, as she and her husband walked down the street.

"Goodnight mami. Wunna sleep fine," Tony replied, as the couple walked out of sight.

Franck was on a date at a new cabaret in town when he read the text. His date was a lovely lady who was a former classmate of his. He told her he had to leave. After apologizing quickly and paying the bill, he picked up his jacket, got into his car, and drove at top speed to Raelynn's house.

There were fire trucks and sirens blazing all around the house when Franck pulled over. As usual, it looked like they came a little too late. The house was up in flames and there was no way the building could be saved. He saw Lum standing by a corner wringing her hands and crying. He rushed up to her.

"Hey. I got your text. What happened?"

"I....I....don't   knowwwwwww.   I   was just…just…in town….nn..nn...." She looked like she was hyperventilating.

"Take a deep breath Lum. Breathe, breathe," he urged, while slowly patting her on the back. She took a few moments to calm down before continuing.

"I was in town with some friends, when one of the neighbors called me and said the house was on fire. She'd already called the police and asked me to get back as fast as I could."

"Is anyone in the house?"

She shook her head. "John and Agnes have the day off."

"What about Rae?"

"She was in the house when I left. One of the firemen rushed in and did a quick swoop of the house. Nobody was in there. She must have left."

"But the car is still parked outside. Where could she have gone? Did you call her?"

"I did." She cried. "It went to voicemail. Do you think she's still in there?"

Franck put both of his hands on his head. He did not like this. Until Raelynn was found, they could not rule out the possibility that she was inside the house. "I don't know. I don't know," was all he said.

Just then, he saw Tony pull up with his car. He quickly climbed out of it and there was a look of abject terror in his eyes. He got out of the car and walked up to them.

"What happened?" he asked. Repeating the same question Franck had asked moments ago. Lum repeated everything she told Franck.

"Do you know what started the fire?" Tony asked.

"No one knows for sure. Their main concern now is putting out the flames. They'll carry out an investigation later."

"Oh man," Tony exclaimed. "Hope she's out of the house. The firefighters can't go in there to double check. It's too risky."

The three of them turned and continued to look at the two-story house that was roaring up in flames.

Raelynn eyes fluttered, as she tried to open her eyes. It was so hot in here; it felt like a furnace. She started coughing violently. She could barely breathe.

The air was thick with smoke. She clutched her bump in distress, as she continued to cough. She tried opening her eyes, but the smoke immediately stung her eyes. She braved the pain, as she looked around to get her bearings. She saw the tiny teddy bear Bryan had given her on their first Valentines Day as a couple, and knew she was under her bed. She slowly crawled out from under it and stood up. There were flames everywhere. She continued coughing violently. As she made her way out of the bedroom and into the corridor, she pulled her shirt up over her mouth to help her breathe. The roof was beginning to cave in from the fire so she had to dodge falling pieces of wood, as she made her way towards the staircase. When she got there, she realized a large beam from the ceiling had fallen down and destroyed half of the staircase. There was no way she would make it out that way.

She was exhausted with all the smoke inhalation. She can't die in here. She had to fight and live, not only for her child, but also so she could avenge Josh's death and make sure Anthony paid for all he had done. There had to be another way out of here. She gathered all her strength and carefully crawled back to her bedroom. At least the roof in there had not caved in. Plus, there was a window inside. In a couple of minutes, which seemed like an eternity, she made it back to her bedroom and closed the door. She was coughing so hard, she was afraid she would cough up a lung. She crawled up to the window. She now heard sirens blasting and a lot of commotion all around the house. She tried to open the window, but it was firmly locked. "Tony must have done that," she thought.

She screamed, "HELP!!!!" but her voice barely sounded; it only made her cough more. She banged on the window with all her might. She looked around for something to break the window. All she found was a long candle-stick holder. She used it in an attempt to break the window. It was an extra double thick glass and it would not budge. Her strength was fading. After a few more thrusts, she slowly slid to the ground and slipped off again into oblivion.

Franck was pacing back and forth in front of the house. He heard something tapping, but with all the noise outside the house, he thought he imagined it. He heard the noise again, this time it sounded like a bang, which repeated every couple of seconds. He looked up at the house and tried to look into the windows amidst the smoke. Then he saw her.

"Oh my goodness! She's up there! She's up there!" he yelled, as he ran towards the lead fireman and pointed to the window. The banging stopped and she disappeared.

The fireman looked up.

"Are you sure Son? I don't see or hear anything."

"She's up there," Franck shouted. "I saw her with my own two eyes. You gotta hurry, I think she passed out."

"Just to be double sure, we'll send a guy up there."

Franck held his breath as the firemen lined up a ladder next to the window where he had seen her.

Two of the fireman climbed up on the ladder. When the first one reached the window, he looked in and saw her sprawled on the floor.

"Sir," he yelled down at his boss. "She's in there! She's in there!"

He tried to break the window with his hands, but it was too thick. He reached down into one of his pockets and grabbed a tiny cooler. He pressed the cooler against the glass until it became brittle and then he hit the glass again with his fist. This time it shattered. He climbed into the window and threw a blanket over her body. He picked her off the floor and gently handed her to the second fireman who gently placed her over his shoulder, as he started climbing back down the ladder. She was still unconscious. Paramedics were waiting for them at the foot of the ladder. When he got to the base, he immediately handed her over to them. The medical team rushed her to the ambulance and placed an oxygen mask over her mouth. They checked her heart rate, as well as that of the fetus. After a couple of minutes, she started coughing--that was a good sign.

Raelynn felt her lungs soak in the wonderful air. She coughed for a while and then she stopped. She smiled weakly. She made it out alive. She opened a fraction of her eyes and saw a bunch of people in a blur swarming around her. She could hear Franck and Lum's voice say, "Rae? Rae? Can you hear us? Are you okay?" She felt someone move up next to her and take her in his arms. She opened her eyes again and blinked, as they swam into focus. She turned and looked up at the person who was holding her in his arms. It was Tony. A murderous look entered her eyes and she squirmed away.

"What is it Babe? You are ok. You are ok. Everything is going to be fine now," he said and tried to bring her into his arms again.

Her eyes opened so wide she thought they would pop out of her head. She put the mask away from her mouth and shouted, "Get away from me you snake! You tried to kill me!" She started coughing again and one of the paramedics quickly pushed the oxygen mask back over her mouth and nose.

"What?" Tony cried, feigning ignorance. "How could you say such a thing? Babe, the smoke and lack of oxygen must have affected some of your brain cells. You are not making any sense."

Raelynn tried to remove the oxygen mask again and fire back at Tony, but the paramedic restrained her and kept the mask on. A policeman in his early fifties walked up to them and asked the paramedic, "Is she feeling alright to answer a few questions?"

"In just a few moments, Sir. Her oxygen levels are really low. They should be back up soon. Everything else looks fine, but we are still going to take her to the hospital to run some tests, and make sure the baby isn't in any kind of distress."

The policeman nodded and waited patiently until the paramedic felt it was okay for Raelynn to take off her mask and talk.

"Young Lady are you feeling well enough to answer a few questions before you head to the hospital?"

"Yes, Officer. That Man," Raelynn responded, as she pointed to Tony, "Tried to kill me."

"That's crazy Officer. I don't know what she's talking about," Tony retorted.

"He's lying. He realized I found out he's the one who murdered my twin brother, Josh Ngwa, and he tried to kill me so no one else would find out the truth."

There were shocked gasps all around them. The officer looked at Tony, then he looked at Raelynn, and then at Tony again.

"I don't know what she's talking about," Tony said. "The smoke inhalation must have confused her a little. I would never do anything like that."

"I have evidence." She pulled out a tiny recording device from inside her bra and handed it to the officer. "You can press play here," she said, showing him a tiny button on the side.

Tony's eyes popped with horror. What was that device? Where did she get all these gadgets? The girl truly had a lot of tricks up her sleeve. He never should have underestimated her. He should have killed her with his bare hands, instead of setting up the fire trying to make it look like an accident.

The officer pressed play and the whole conversation they had earlier replayed. He was toast. Although he knew it probably would not make any difference, he got up, and started running like the wind. Unfortunately for him, before he ran ten meters, two police officers caught him and pushed him to the ground.

"Mr. Anthony Mbah. You are under arrest for the murder of Josh Ngwa and attempted murder of Raelynn Ngwa," the lead officer said, as they dragged him off to the police car.

Eleven

Raelynn stood at the iron door and lifted her hand to knock on the door. She lost her nerve and dropped it. She contemplated whether she should really be here when the door swung open.

"Raelynn!!! I thought I saw you from the window. "Come on in."

Raelynn gave Laura a feeble smile as she walked in through the door.

"Nice place you got here," Raelynn said weakly.

"Oh yeah, thanks. The state gave me some money after my release, as some sort of compensation. I wanted to find a new place to start over again, you know. The other one had to many bad memories."

Raelynn agreed with her. She would not want to sleep in the house where Josh was murdered either; -- even if she got paid. It felt haunted. She wondered why Laura was being so friendly with her. The last time they saw one another was in court, when Laura was wrongly convicted for Josh's murder and sentenced to fifty years in prison. She felt no remorse for her at the time and watched with glee, as Laura was dragged off to jail.

"Please have a seat," Laura suggested, interrupting her musings. "Would you like anything to eat or drink?"

"No thanks. I'm good," Raelynn answered and took a seat on the dark sofa. Laura took a seat next to her and for a moment, they sat in silence.

"So what brings you by?" Laura finally asked.

Raelynn cleared her throat and started sobbing. "Ummmm…mm…mm. I don't even know where to begin. I know this may mean nothing to you now, but I'm so sorry Laura. For everything. I now know you loved Josh almost as much as I did, and it kills me that I made you go through so much pain. I will spend the rest of my life making it up to you. I hope you can find room in your heart to forgive me."

Laura gently smiled and reached over to grab one of her hands. "It's all forgiven Rae. Don't worry about it. People make mistakes and given the circumstances, anyone would have thought I was guilty. I trusted God to deliver me, and He did. That's all in the past now."

"Really?"

"Yeah really. It's all forgiven."

"Just like that? Why are you being so nice to me, when all I ever did was hurt you?" Laura gave her that gentle smile again. "Believe me, it's not by my power, but it's by the grace of God."

Raelynn gave her a confused look. Laura explained, "See God has forgiven me of all my sins and shortcomings. 'He sent His only Son Jesus Christ to die on the cross for my sins' from Romans 3:25 of the New International Version (NIV). He has blessed me in so many ways; I can't even begin to name them all. I 'didn't deserve His grace and mercy' from Hebrews 4:16 of the New International Version (NIV); all I had to do was accept it. Just like He forgave all my transgressions, I'm able to do the same for other people."

Raelynn sniffed and looked directly into Laura's eyes. That was so crazy. She never met anyone like Laura before. If roles were reversed, she would have punched Laura if she showed up at her doorstep. There was something different about her; a peace and tranquility about her that money could not buy. She wanted what Laura had. She wanted to let go of all the pain, bitterness, and resentment in her life. Something tugged at her heart, a voice calling her to go home. A yearning that had been there for a long time, yet she ignored it. "Yeah I've heard about Him. He sounds like a pretty cool Guy."

"The best. He's a good, good, Father."

"Would He…He," Raelynn stammered. Would this God that both Bryan and now Laura talked about really want her? She was so broken. "Would He be interested in someone like me?"

"Of course Rae. We are all His creation. He accepts and loves all of us, just as we are."

"But I've done some pretty bad things."

It doesn't matter. He still loves you. 'There is nothing that can separate us from the love of Christ'," from Romans 8:31-39 of the New Living Translation (NLT).

"Even though I was a thief, and stole thousands of dollars from hundreds of people?"

"He still loves you."

"Even if I might be a fugitive?"

"He still loves you."

"Even though I abandoned my husband and got a divorce?"

"He still loves you."

"Even though, I am pregnant out of wedlock with my brother's murderer?"

"He still loves you. 'For all have sinned and fallen short of the glory of God', from Romans 3:23 of the King James Version (KJV). 'His grace is sufficient to wipe away all our sins; even the darkest ones'," from 2 Corinthians 12:9 of the King James Version (KJV).

Raelynn buried her hands in her face and wept. The tug she felt became stronger. A yearning for a God so wonderful and forgiving; there was nothing she could do that would make Him hate her.

"I want Him in my life," she finally said.

"'Do you believe that you are sinner? And that Jesus Christ died for your sins?'" From Romans 10:9 of the New King James Version (NKJV).

"Yes I do."

Laura took Raelynn's hands in both of her own and said, "Repeat this prayer after me,

'Lord Jesus,

I confess that you are the Son of God,
that you died for my sins and rose again on the
third day.
I accept you this day as my personal Lord and
Savior.
Come into my life and take control, make me a
better person.
I want to live my life for you.
From today, I forsake all my sinful ways
And dedicate myself to the glory of God
Amen."'

After Raelynn repeated the prayer, Laura gave her a warm hug. "Welcome to the fam, Sis." Raelynn hugged her back tightly, as she shed tears of joy.

Since it was a Saturday evening, Laura coaxed Raelynn into spending the night at her place and going to church with her the following morning. They barely slept that night, because they stayed up all night and talked about everything. Raelynn told her about Madame Josephine and her gang (nobody else in Cameroon knew, not even Franck). She also told her about Bryan and their divorce. They fondly talked about Josh and each of their shared memories of him. When they went to Laura's church the next day, Raelynn was nervous. She could not remember the last time she went to the church. Everyone welcomed her and was kind. She truly felt she was amongst family.

During the sermon, the pastor preached on the resurrection of Lazarus in John 11 from the King James Version (KJV). Just as Lazarus was brought back to life, believers need to die to themselves and their sinful ways and be born again--resurrected as a new person in Christ. Often times, just as Lazarus was bound with wrappings and had to be untied, Christians who are born again are often still bound to things of their old life and need to be cut off from those things. It was a powerful sermon, and as a new Christian, she wondered what things from her old life were still binding her.

Throughout the following week, Raelynn felt a tug in her heart to take all the money she and Josh made illegally and give to the poor. It was not until she read about Zacchaeus the tax collector in Luke 19:1-10 from the King James Version (KJV), that she made up her mind. She reached out to all the charity organizations she could find and gave back all the money they made from conning people. She wanted no part of the money anymore. After she had done this, she felt so much peace.

6 weeks later

"I'm going on a Baby Moon!" Raelynn announced as she, Lum, and Tita were at Franck's place for dinner.

"Baby Moon?" asked Tita. "What's that?"

"It's a little holiday the parents or expectant mother takes before the baby is born," Lum answered for her.

"Where are you going?" Franck asked.

"South Africa. Specifically Pretoria, and Cape Town."

"Oooo that sounds lovely. I've heard South Africa is so beautiful," Lum said.

"Can you even afford it?" Franck asked skeptically. "I thought you gave away all your money."

"Well, not really. I kept 50% of the company. We were under the water for a few weeks, but the new manager is doing an awesome job. We are making a profit again. I can afford the trip. And given everything that has happened, I need to get away for a little bit and relax."

"When are you due? Will they let you fly?" Tita asked.

"Yeah of course. I have two more months. I'm not even showing that much," Raelynn said, as she rubbed her small baby bump. She really did not look like she was seven months pregnant.

"Are you going by yourself? Do you even know anyone there?" Franck asked with concern.

"Nahh. It's just me."

"Is that even safe?"

"Franck, please. What's the worse that could happen? It's not like I'm going into the middle of Syria or something. South Africa has been safe for decades. It's even safer than Cameroon right now."

Franck shrugged. "I'm just concerned about you Rae, that's all."

Raelynn smiled and reached out to pat him on the shoulder. "I know you are Franck and I appreciate it. Don't worry about me. I'm a big girl."

"Well I hope you have fun and get refreshed. When are you leaving?"

"In three days."

"Oh wow!" Lum exclaimed. "Go have fun girl."

Three days later, Raelynn walked out of Cape Town International Airport and hailed a cab. A taxi driver in his thirties pulled over and helped her get her small suitcase into the trunk of the taxi. Packing had been so easy, since she did not own as many clothes anymore. Most of them were destroyed in the fire. Since she was only visiting for a couple of days, she had no need to do any major shopping for clothes.

As the driver drove along, he chatted nonstop. He pointed at some of the major tourist spots in the area and mentioned a bunch of restaurants she had to try out. When he pulled up in front of the Bay Hotel thirty minutes later, she knew so much about the town's history and culture that she could write an essay on it. She got out of the cab, grabbed her luggage, and headed for the reception desk. The woman at the counter was super friendly and soon gave her the keys to her room.

When she got to her room on the fifteenth floor and opened the door, she gave out a sigh of relief. It was perfect. There was a single queen bed with white sheets and a dark red comforter. The carpet was eggshell white and so was all the furniture in the room. But the most beautiful thing about the room was the view. There was a sliding door, which led to a small balcony, which overlooked the Atlantic Ocean. Rae opened the sliding door and walked onto the balcony and breathed in the fresh air. She smelled the ocean and heard the soothing sounds of the waves in the distance. She closed her eyes and stood there for a long time. Letting her senses soak in all that was there.

It was getting dark, so she went back inside and took a shower. She put on a stripped overflowing sundress and went out to find dinner. Fortunately, there were lots of restaurants around, so she did not have to take a cab. She Googled one, which was a five-minute walk from her hotel.

She ordered Bobotie, a South African delicacy that is baked and consists of minced meat simmered with curry powder, herbs and dried fruit, topped with a mixture of egg and milk. It was so good. She ate until she could barely walk. When she made it back to her room, she reached for her Bible and climbed in bed. Laura told her it was essential for her as a Christian to spend time everyday with the Lord and ask for the Holy Spirit to fill her so He would direct her in every aspect of her life.

Over the past few weeks, she had read many books in the Bible. She wanted to catch up on all she had missed. She read the books of the Bible as though she was reading a novel, and she did not really meditate on any passages. Laura cautioned her not to rush through each passage, but to meditate and reflect on all the words she read.

She opened her Bible to 1 Samuel and started reading about the story of David. He was one of her favorite Bible characters. She read the part where he fled from King Saul. All of a sudden, she got this weird feeling she should leave that hotel and move to another one. "Was this the Holy Spirit talking to her?" No, she thought and shook her head. "Why would the Holy Spirit tell her to do something like that? It made no sense. This hotel was perfectly fine and she absolutely loved it. It couldn't be the Holy Spirit." She ignored the feeling and closed her Bible.

She turned on the TV and browsed through the channels for an interesting movie to watch. She settled for the classic movie, *Pretty Woman*, with Julia Roberts and Richard Gere. At some point during the movie, she dozed off and didn't wake up till 2:30 am, when she felt the baby kicking. He normally kicked a lot, but this time, it was a lot stronger and so much more painful. She took in some deep breaths, as she learned to do in the Lamaze class to help relieve the pain. About fifteen minutes later, the kicking subsided, and she was able to fall back asleep.

She did not wake up until 10:00 am in the morning. She would have continued sleeping, but the baby was apparently very hungry and so was she. She needed to find food right away. She took a quick shower before rushing out. As she left, she saw there was a lot of commotion at the hotel's entrance. There was an international conference going on in Pretoria and a lot of people from other countries were filling up the vacant rooms within the hotels in the area. She saw some Americans, as well as Europeans trying to book a room. She was going to ask one of the hotel workers what was going on, but she was too hungry to really care, so she walked on.

She went to the same restaurant she went to the day before and got a simple breakfast of whole grain toast with eggs, cheese and bacon, some tea and the local fruit. After breakfast, she walked to the beach and lay under one of the beach chairs for a while. She later took a long walk along the beach and watched people surfing and swimming in the clear water, sunbathing, playing beach volleyball and all other fun beach activities.

It wasn't until it got dark that she made her way back to her hotel room. She had a full day and was thoroughly exhausted. The hotel was now fully occupied. There were many people in the lobby, elevators, and hallways. If she paid a little more attention, she would have noticed many of the people in the hotel were either models or their agents. But she was too hungry and exhausted to notice. She had been on her feet a lot longer than usual for a woman in her condition.

After she showered, she sat up on her bed and ate some curry-fried rice she picked up from one of the street vendors at the beach. As the night before, she put on the TV and chose a random show. She instantly fell asleep.

She awoke slowly and saw a blur of two figures standing at the door. She thought she was dreaming, so she closed her eyes again for a moment before opening them again. This time the image was clearer and she saw a couple standing at the door. Who could they possibly be? Her eyes immediately shot open and she sat up startled. Her eyes almost popped from her head. When the sleep cleared from her eyes, she recognized the couple.

"Hello *Ma Petite*," Madame Josephine said in a pleasant voice. Raelynn drew in air to scream, when Derrick pulled out a gun from under his jacket and pointed it directly at her chest.

"Don't even think about it," he said in a drawl voice. Raelynn swallowed and kept quiet. She edged to the headboard of the bed and looked at them with panic. She began to recite in her head one of the first Bible verses Laura asked her to memorize. It was from Psalms 23, of the King James Version (KJV), 'The Lord is my Shepherd, I shall not want. He maketh me to lie down in green pastures: he leadeth me beside the still waters…'

"Now, now, *Ma Puce*. You look frightened to death," Madame Josephine said with a throaty laugh. "As well as you should be. You know what I do to anyone who double crosses me, right?"

Raelynn nodded her head vigorously in agreement. '… He restoreth my soul: he leadeth me in the paths of righteousness for his name's sake.'

"*Tres bien*. I'm sure you are wondering how we managed to find you. Honestly, I didn't waste an ounce of my time looking for you after you vanished. I made a promise to myself that if I ever saw you again, I'd make you pay. Today, the opportunity presented itself nicely. Derrick and I came into town yesterday for a fashion event. To our surprise, one of my associates said they saw you in this hotel's lobby area earlier this morning. It didn't take much to confirm that information and get your room number. So here we are."

"What are you gonna do to me?" '...Yea, though I walk through the valley of the shadow of death, I will fear no evil: for thou art with me; thy rod and thy staff they comfort me.'

"Well you know... if we were in America, I would have worked on something more elaborate. But since we are in a foreign country and this was kinda sudden, I'll have to improvise. *Juste un peu.* Now get up."

Raelynn slowly climbed out of the bed. Derrick walked up to her and barked, "Move." He roughly pulled her towards one the chairs in the room and shoved her down onto it, while pointing the gun at her head. Madame Josephine pulled a rope out of her purse and tied Raelynn firmly to the chair. When she was done, she pulled off a pillowcase from one of the pillows and gagged her with it.

"There we go. We are all set," Madame Josephine said taking a step back. "Ohh Raelynn, I wished you hadn't crossed me like that. You were one of my favorites. But a promise is a debt. No one double crosses me."

She held out her hand to Derrick to hand her the gun. She pointed the gun at Raelynn's stomach and fired. The gun had a silencer on it, so it did not make a sound. Both Raelynn and the baby inside her belly flinched back in pain. Tears streamed down her eyes. The baby was in severe trauma and Raelynn could feel his pain.

Madame Josephine handed the gun back to Derrick and walked up to her, "Hmmm *Ma Petite*, I don't think the little one will make it. This should teach you a lesson, and give you a lot to think about if you stay alive. I doubt you will, but just in case you do, don't you dare mention my name or company. If you do, someone will return to finish the job." Madame Josephine then leaned down and placed a soft kiss on Raelynn's forehead. "*Arrevoir Ma Puce.*" She nodded at Derrick, and they quietly left the room, leaving Raelynn bleeding on the chair.

Raelynn sat soaked in blood. "God please help me and my baby," she cried. She tried to wriggle free from the binding rope, but she could not loosen the rope.. She became progressively weaker from the blood loss. She used her feet and shuffled the chair across the room. The friction of the carpet made it a lot more difficult. After moving a couple of inches, she could not move anymore. She tried to scream for help, but the gag was so secure no sound escaped her lips. "Why wouldn't God save her," she wondered. Was this pay back for all the wrongs she had before? She thought He had forgiven her from all of her sins. She felt her eyes drooping. "Lord save us," was her final thought before she slipped off into unconsciousness.

***

The next time her eyes fluttered open, she saw a lot of people in scrubs. She sensed she was on a stretcher, as they pulled her along.

"Come on Ma'am," one of the doctors or nurses yelled. "Stay with me! Stay with me!"

"She's lost a lot of blood," another doctor shouted out to someone. "Get me two units of blood type O."

"Her pulse is getting weaker."

"I'm not getting anything from the fetus. We need to get her to an OR immediately. Page Dr. Botha right away."

"We are losing her again. Call…" Their voices faded as she slipped back into unconsciousness.

When her eyes fluttered again, she was lying on a bed in a hospital room. The room had white walls and a blue floor. There was a huge window to her right, and a sliding door to her left. There was heavy machinery around her bed. She could not completely make out what they were. There was also a tan couch behind the window, facing her. Right now, there was a young doctor with her white coat on, sitting on the couch, taking notes. She felt ridiculously sluggish that it took great efforts to keep her eyes open even for a fraction of a second. She closed them again and slept.

The next time she opened her eyes, she was still very sluggish, but felt strong enough to fully open her eyes. Reflexively, she reached down and touched her baby bump. It was gone.

"W…wh…what? W…wh…where is…?" she mumbled with a hoarse voice. Her throat was so dry. She tried to sit up. A nurse standing in the hallway immediately rushed in and pushed her shoulders back down onto the bed.

"No, no Ma'am. Don't move too much. You'll remove your stitches. How are you feeling?" the nurse asked and began to check her vital signs from a monitor, which was one of the machines connected to Raelynn.

Raelynn laid one hand on her throat and said, "Thirsty."

The nurse picked up a cup of water with a straw from a nearby table, and held it for her while she took a few sips. "Is that better Ma'am?"

Raelynn nodded and said in a stronger voice, "Yeah, thanks. What happened to my baby?"

"I'll get the doctor," the nurse replied and left abruptly. A few moments later, the nurse came back, accompanied by a doctor in his middle or late forties. His eyes were kind as he smiled at her.

"Ms. Ngwa. I'm Dr. Botha. I'm so glad to see you awake. How are you feeling? Any pain?"

"A little. Not too much. I just feel very sluggish. How long have I been out?"

"You've been unconscious for three days. The sluggishness is mostly from the narcotics we've been giving you. Gunshot wounds, especially in the abdomen, can be extremely painful. Now that you are conscious, we will reduce the dosage and see how it goes, ok?"

Raelynn nodded.

"Try not to move too much," Dr. Botha added. "If not, your stitches will rip, and we will have to redo them." He walked closer to her bed and examined her. "Everything looks good, Ms. Ngwa. Do you know who shot you?"

Raelynn shook her head.

"Well, the police are investigating your attack. One of them will debrief you once they return back to check on you."

"Thanks Doc. What happened to my baby?"

Dr. Botha and the nurse gave each other a look. "Well, that can't be good," Raelynn thought.

"Ms. Ngwa, I'm afraid I have some bad news. Do you have any family or friends we can call for you? It is better to be in the company of loved ones, when we deliver the news."

Raelynn shook her head. "No, I don't have any family and friends here. I am on vacation by myself."

"That's too bad. I'm so sorry Miss. "He took in a deep breath. "There's no easy way to say this. We tried everything we could, but we couldn't revive the baby. The bullet hit the baby directly in the chest. He lost so much blood that his heart stopped beating. I'm so sorry for your loss."

Raelynn's heart clutched in sorrow and tears ran unchecked down her face. Josh was no more. The loss of her son felt like she was reliving the loss of her brother. Only this time, it was her fault he died. If she only stayed in Cameroon. If only she had moved out of that hotel when she felt that tug.

"Unfortunately, there is more, Miss," Dr. Botha continued. How could there be more? What could be worse than her little boy's death? "The baby lost a lot of blood before we could remove him. This severely damaged your uterus. The Obstetrics and Gynecology team did everything they could for your uterus. They were able to repair it enough so we didn't have to completely remove it. There is a lot of scarring on the uterus, which implies your chances are very slim of you ever getting pregnant again. I am so sorry."

Raelynn turned her head away from the doctor and looked out the window; that was something else to mourn about; she filed it away for later. For now, she would mourn the loss of her baby boy.

Twelve

Raelynn looked down at the crashing waves from the cliffs of Cape Point. There was a strong breeze, which made her clothes flap around her. She clutched the small purple sweater she wore. She could actually see the line where the Pacific and Atlanta oceans met. It was spectacular!

She was discharged from the hospital earlier that morning and had somehow wandered out here. The past two weeks seemed like a haze. She woke up crying and went to sleep crying. Even in her sleep, nightmares haunted her. It was a variation of one of two dreams.

In the first one, Josh was hanging off a cliff. She offered him her hand so she could pull him up, but just as their fingers touched, he lost his grip and fell into a huge canyon. It was very similar to the dream she'd had about Josh the night he was murdered. In the second dream, she heard a baby (her baby) crying, but it was so foggy she could not find him. She searched and searched, but to no avail. The baby's cries lessened and eventually stopped; she was alone.

The doctor and nurses attending to her and did their best to console her. They took rounds chatting with and hanging out with her and making jokes. They offered to call her family in Cameroon, but she flatly declined. Who was there to call? She had no real family left, except for Ma Bridget. She was an old woman who needed to be left in peace. Thanks to Raelynn, the rest of her family was all gone.

'Why don't you join them?' a tiny voice said in her head.

'No, no. Don't do that.' Another voice said. 'You have so much to live for.' Raelynn shook her head as she looked down from the steep cliffs. The drop had to be at least a hundred meters.

'You've already suffered so much. Don't you think it's time for you to go and rest?'

'I know this seems hard, but trust Me it will get better.'

'Do you really believe that? Things might only get worse. You are a walking time bomb.'

"The first voice is right," Raelynn thought. "What could this life possibly have to offer?" It had brought her nothing but sorrow and pain.

Ending it all was so simple really. All she has to do is slide off the edge of one of those rocks and in less than a minute, it will all be over. She'll be in a place with no more pain, no more sorrow. She thought about writing a note and then scoffed. Nobody will really care. Franck, Lum, Tita, Rita and all her extended family and friends might be shocked, but in time, they'll forget her. She brought nothing but misery into their lives anyways.

She took a deep breath and stood over the edge of one of the rocks. This is it. Just then she heard someone shout, "RAELYNN!"

"Bryan?" She wondered. "No it couldn't be." This was her mind playing games with her. She put one foot over the edge when she heard, "RAELYNN! STOP!" With one foot still hanging in the air, she turned her head in the direction of the yelling and saw Bryan running towards her. He stopped a couple of inches away from her, panting and looking directly into her eyes.

Raelynn could not believe she would ever see her ex-husband, particularly at a time like this. Either God has a funny sense of humor or Bryan was yet another reminder of all the people she hurt. Was he brought here to reinforce her choice to jump?

"Bryan? What are you doing here?"

"I could ask you the same thing. What are you doing?"

"What does it look like I'm doing?" She looked down at the cliff again. It seemed so very enticing now. "I'm done."

"Rae please, don't. I'm begging you."

"How did you even find me? Why are you here?"

"I came here for a business trip. Something led me to come here today; and I'm just in time, I see. Please Rae, don't jump."

"Why do you even care?"

"Because you are my wife. But more importantly, you are one of God's children and He doesn't want you to do this. This is murder, Rae."

"I'm your wife?" She asked incredulously. "What are you talking about Bryan? We got a divorce."

"You gave me divorce papers to sign. I never signed them. I actually tore them up. So there you go. We are still married."

Tears filled her eyes. "Why?"

"Because I loved you then, Rae. And I still do," he said earnestly. "I wasn't willing to give up on our marriage just like that."

"Why?" she asked again. "I haven't done anything to deserve your love. I initially set out to ruin you, I lied to you for years and I abandoned our marriage. And that's just the part you know, there's a lot more. Believe me Bryan, you don't want to love a woman like me. I bring nothing but trouble."

"I don't believe that."

"Well, it's the truth."

"It doesn't matter what you did, so long as we are still willing to work on our marriage."

"How can you say that? Are you trying to tell me my leaving didn't hurt you at all?" she sniffed.

Bryan took a deep breath. He had not seen her in almost a year. Initially, he had felt so hurt and betrayed that he wanted nothing to do with her. He even tried putting the torn divorce papers together and going through with the divorce, to no avail. Eventually he had forgiven her and prayed that they would reconnect. All he wanted to do now was put his arms around her and give her a hug.

"How can you ask a question like that? Of course I was hurt. Badly. I was devastated. I locked myself up in my apartment for days. It was only the grace of God and the counseling of my mentor that helped me to get back on my feet."

"I'm so sorry Bryan for all the pain I put you through. Leaving you was one of the hardest things I have ever done in my life."

"Rae, I forgave you for that a long time ago. Will you please just get away from the edge of that cliff?"

"You know the other reason why I left New York suddenly?" she blurted out. He shook his head no. "Franck called and told me Josh was missing."

Bryan shook his head no again." I'm sorry Rae, I had no idea. I tried contacting Josh after you left, but he didn't get any of my messages. Why didn't you tell me Rae? I could have helped you."

"I thought that after I told you I was a criminal, you wouldn't want anything to do with me, much less help me find my brother. So I took the coward's way out and left you before you could leave me."

"Rae….that's just…"

"I know Bryan. It was so stupid and cowardly."

"I think I understand your leaving a little more now," he said thoughtfully. "But Rae, you gotta understand nothing you do will ever make me stop loving you. We are married; for better or for worse. As long as there is a slim chance of making our marriage work again, I will take that shot."

"Awww, you are so sweet. You might not feel the same way when I'm done with my story."

"What happened to Josh? Where you able to find him?"

"Yup, a month later. He was murdered."

Bryan gasped. "Oh my goodness!!! What??? Josh is dead? Rae...I am so sorry." He tried walking closer to her but she held a hand up. He stopped right where he was.

"Just lemme finish please. I made my peace with it, a while ago, but set out to seek revenge. I had Josh's girlfriend arrested, who turned out to be innocent. Then I got pregnant by his business partner, who turned out to be the murderer."

Bryan closed his eyes and tried to process what she said; it was too much. He ran a hand over his head and face. Raelynn's heart sank again. She never thought she could hurt him any more than she already had. Apparently she still could.

"You...you... you slept with another guy?" he stammered.

Raelynn put her foot down and sank to her knees and buried her face into her hands, weeping profusely. "I'm sorry Bryan. It was only one time. I just found out Josh was dead. I wasn't thinking straight and he came to console me and...and...I don't know what happened. Still, it is no excuse." She dropped her hands and looked at him with teary eyes. "I told you I was a bad person."

"Rae, you are not a bad person. Everyone makes mistakes. From what I understand, the guy is a scoundrel. You were vulnerable and in a bad place and this guy took advantage of you. And you got pregnant from the single encounter?" She nodded.

"Did you say you found out later he murdered your twin?" She nodded again

"Wow!" Bryan exclaimed and put his hands on his waist. Talk about a bad break. He wondered what she had done with the pregnancy, cause she sure didn't look pregnant now. Did she already have the baby? Or had she aborted it? He wanted to ask, but felt it would be better if she volunteered to tell him the information herself.

"After I found out the truth about Josh's murder, I became a Christian. I gave my life to Christ," she continued. He wanted to shout, 'Ohh really? That's great.' But he felt a nudging from the Holy Spirit to keep quiet and let her continue.

"Then I came out here for a brief vacation before the baby came. Guess who finds me here? Madame Josephine and her minion. They murder my baby boo, attempt to kill me and left me infertile."

Bryan was so shocked he stared at her, and barely spoke. She saw a single tear roll down his right cheek.

"See I thought I had given my life to God who loves me and could forgive all my sins, but it turns out He doesn't love me and He hasn't forgiven me. He hates me in fact."

"Oh my goodness!!! I can't believe this Rae. I don't even know what to say. I'm so sorry and I wish I could have been there for you. More than you realize. But God doesn't hate you. He loves you very, very, much. You are His anointed daughter."

"Then why would He allow so many bad things to happen to me? Why would He take my baby boy?

Why could He not save him? I'm just so tired of all the pain Bryan. I just want to rest."

"Rae, the world is broken, I know. Since Adam and Eve fell and sin entered the world, it was broken. But God leaves us in this earth for a purpose and when it's time for Him to call us home, He will. But we can't just leave without accomplishing our purpose. When we go through pain and trials in this world, God is only allowing us to go through it for a season, so we can become stronger and learn to depend on Him more. Sometimes, bad things happen because there are consequences for the sins we commit. God can wash away every sin, but we still have to deal with the consequences of our actions. Do you know King David's story in the Bible?" She nodded. "See after David committed adultery with Bathsheba and then committed murder, later he repented. God forgave him. But the child they had together still died and there was a lot of calamity in his house because of those sins. Maybe some of the bad things that happened to you are just consequences of some other things you did. But God still loves you, passionately. And like David, you have to continue to trust Him. He can make all things new. Just have faith in Him."

"I have no one Bryan. Nobody cares if I live or die."

"What are you talking about? I just told you I love you," Bryan cried out.

"You still love me?" she asked incredulously. "After everything I told you? Do you realize I may never be able to have a child again?"

"Yeah Rae, I realize that. It doesn't matter. I still love you. My love for you is unconditional. The day we got married, and the day I gave my life to Christ, I decided and chose to love you till the day I die. I love you as Christ loves His church and gave His life for it."

"But I don't deserve it. I really don't. How can you love broken goods like me?"

"The love I have for you isn't dependent on whether you think you deserve it or not. And you are not broken goods. Things may seem bleak now, but the God we serve is a God of restoration. We can never be too broken for Him to fix and restore us. You may be down now, but I believe if you put your trust in Him, He will make you rise again."

"You really believe that?"

"Yeah I do, with all my heart. There are only two answers I need to know; do you still love me? Is there any part of you willing to fight for our marriage?"

She was sobbing uncontrollably now. "I love you Bryan. I always have, and I always will. If you can accept me just as I am with all my past and my failures, I'm willing to take this chance with you; to entrust our lives to God; to find our purpose in this life; to be your wife and serve you till the day I die."

Bryan sniffed and held out his hand to her. She took it and rose to her feet. He then pulled her into an embrace and they both cried as they held onto each other tightly. "God really had never abandoned her," Raelynn thought. He sent Bryan at just the right moment, to save her from herself.

God may not come when you want Him to, but He is always on time.

Epilogue

Eighteen Months Later

Raelynn and Bryan once again stood on the cliffs of Cape Point holding hands in front of a group of people. It was the same place where she tried to commit suicide. It was also the same place where she and Bryan had reunited. Over the past months, this place had become special to both of them. They came here often to spend quiet time with the Lord and meditate on all the good things He had done.

They were now rededicating their marriage to the Lord, in front of family and friends. It was a simple yet elegant ceremony. A stand had been made for the pastor and the couple, while the audience sat on white folding back chairs. There was a band in the corner of the stage playing softly. A red carpet was laid from the center stage to the middle where the audience sat.

The folding chairs in the aisles had peach, white and pink lilies taped to them.

Their wedding three years ago was a cozy destination wedding in the Dominican Republic with only a few members of Bryan's family. At this rededication, they invited all their family and friends from Cameroon, Nigeria, United States and South Africa (where they now lived). Franck, Tita, Lum, Ma Bridget, Rita, Bree, Laura, and a few of her other friends were in the audience.

Over the past few months, she began counseling with a Christian psychologist to talk about her issues of guilt, deceit, grief, unworthiness, anger, etc. She was so grateful for her counselors, she is learning to let go of all negative emotions that she had been building for several years. She and Bryan also receive marriage counseling with a Christian pastor in Cape Town. Although Bryan had forgiven her for sleeping with another guy, he was having a hard time forgetting, which affected their physical intimacy as a couple. Going to marriage counseling helped tremendously, and their marriage was doing better than ever.

"Now do you, Bryan Okoye, in front of God, your family and friends, promise to continue to love your wife, comfort her, honor and protect her, forsaking all others, be faithful to her, as long as you both shall live?" the preacher said.

"I will," Bryan replied and grinned broadly at her. She grinned back at him. They made an attractive couple. She wore a simple white dress with her hair styled in an afro bun with flowers around it. She looked beautiful. It was her inner peace that radiated through her and made her glow. He looked dashing too. Dressed in a white suit and a blue cravat.

"Do you, Raelynn Ngwa Okoye, in front of God, your family and friends, promise to continue to love your husband, comfort him, honor and protect him, forsaking all others, be faithful to him, as long as you both shall live?"

"I will."

"Bryan, repeat after me," the preacher said. "I have taken you to be my wife, to have and to hold, for better, for worse, for richer, for poorer, in sickness and in health, to love and to cherish, till death do us part, according to God's holy law, and today I affirm this my solemn promise."

After Bryan repeated, the congregation cheered.

"Raelynn, now repeat after me. I have taken you to be my husband, to have and to hold, for better, for worse, for richer, for poorer, in sickness and in health, to love and to cherish, till death do us part, according to God's holy law, and today I affirm this my solemn promise."

The audience cheered again after Raelynn repeated the vows.

The preacher called for the ring bearer with the rings. "Now both of you repeat after me, 'this ring is a sign of our marriage. With my body I honor you. All that I am I give to you and all that I have I share with you, with the love of God, the Father, the Son and the Holy Spirit.'"

They each slipped a ring on the other's finger.

"Now you may kiss your wife."

Bryan locked arms around her and gave her a passionate kiss, which made the audience cheer and hoot. Raelynn was never so happy in her entire life. She has a husband who truly loves her and she was living her God-given purpose. She started a ministry for girls, who never knew their fathers to help them understand they had a good, good, Father, who will never abandon them. She also started a ministry for women who lost their children. She enjoyed encouraging and helping each woman go through her own painful season. Her ministry prospered and soon would become an international ministry. She traveled around the country, performing speaking engagements, speaking on radio and TV shows to encourage women and girls. Her life had never been as rewarding as it was now. God made her rise again. It was better than anything she ever imagined before. Even if she never had kids, her life was complete and she was genuinely happy.

Seven years later

Raelynn lay on the hospital bed drenched in sweat, trying to catch her breath. She had never been so exhausted in her life. Bryan clutched her hand and leaned over to kiss the top of her head.

"C'mon Babe, you are almost there. Just one more push."

Raelynn could not believe she was in a delivery room about to have twins. She did not believe it seven months ago when the pregnancy test said she was pregnant. She did not even believe it when she went to the hospital and the doctors confirmed her pregnancy. It was only after the first sonogram that it sunk in she was having twins. She wept for joy. Even the doctors were amazed. She was not pregnant with one child, but with twins! Her womb was so scarred it was a miracle the zygotes managed to implant and grow.

Throughout the pregnancy, Raelynn was half expecting a miscarriage or something to go wrong. There was a scare or two, but the pregnancy went well and the babies were doing great. She prayed throughout the pregnancy for a safe and healthy delivery. Bryan also prayed earnestly. During her forty-hour labor, he prayed non-stop covering her and the twins over and over again with the precious blood of Jesus.

"Alright Mrs. Okoye, you are doing great. The baby is crowning. Just one more push," the doctor said.

Raelynn gave a very hard push and the first baby came out. It was a girl. She was screaming at the top of her lungs.

"Oh my gosh, Babe we have a girl, we have a girl!" Bryan yelled with tears in his eyes.

The doctor gave Bryan a pair of scissors to cut the umbilical cord and then handed the baby to a nurse for examination.

"Alright Mrs. Okoye, we are almost there. Good job. Give me one more big push."

Bryan braced her up with an arm around her back as she gave one big final push and another baby came out. It was a boy. And like his sister, he was screaming at the top of his lungs. After his umbilical cord was cut, the nurse whisked him away to examine him.

Raelynn lay back on the bed with relief.

"You did it Babe. I'm so proud of you. I love you," Bryan said softly and kissed her hair.

The nurse brought the twins to her, "Here you are," she said, as she lay each of them in her arms. "Congratulations! Your babies are both doing well."

Raelynn looked at the beautiful babies in her arms and tears filled her eyes. They were truly a miracle. God gave her all she could ever think, dream or even ask for.

STAY CONNECTED
WITH THE AUTHOR

Instagram: dr_cherylinspires
Twitter: dr_cherinspires